As long as Madison was alive, there was still time to save her.

"This is all good news," Knox said, his breath blowing against Jen's hair. "The lab will send folks down here to make casts of the shoe prints for analysis. They'll come back with height and weight estimates of her abductor. Tech will work on getting her phone unlocked. And with a little luck, the security camera recorded the whole thing."

Jen pulled herself together and stepped away. Everyone had a job to do. Including her. She just needed her marching orders. "What now?"

"Now we wait another few minutes for the crime scene team to arrive. Then you and I will take D.J. home and wait for more news. Sound good?"

"Okay."

Knox wrapped his arm across her shoulders, pulling her close as they moved toward his truck.

The warmth of him soothed her, and she allowed herself to breathe easier. Whatever happened next, at least she wasn't alone.

ACCIDENTAL WITNESS

Julie Anne Lindsey

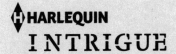

For Jen Jen

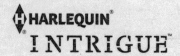

Recycling programs
for this product may
not exist in your area.

ISBN-13: 978-1-335-48953-1

Accidental Witness

Copyright © 2022 by Julie Anne Lindsey

This edition published by arrangement with Harlequin Books S.A.

For questions and comments about the quality of this book,
please contact us at CustomerService@Harlequin.com.

Harlequin Enterprises ULC
22 Adelaide St. West, 41st Floor
Toronto, Ontario M5H 4E3, Canada
www.Harlequin.com

Printed in U.S.A.

Julie Anne Lindsey is an obsessive reader who was once torn between the love of her two favorite genres: toe-curling romance and chew-your-nails suspense. Now she gets to write both for Harlequin Intrigue. When she's not creating new worlds, Julie can be found carpooling her three kids around northeastern Ohio and plotting with her shamelessly enabling friends. Winner of the Daphne du Maurier Award for Excellence in Mystery/Suspense, Julie is a member of International Thriller Writers, Romance Writers of America and Sisters in Crime. Learn more about Julie and her books at julieannelindsey.com.

Books by Julie Anne Lindsey

Harlequin Intrigue

Heartland Heroes

SVU Surveillance
Protecting His Witness
Kentucky Crime Ring
Stay Hidden
Accidental Witness

Fortress Defense

Deadly Cover-Up
Missing in the Mountains
Marine Protector
Dangerous Knowledge

Garrett Valor

Shadow Point Deputy
Marked by the Marshal

Impact Zone

Visit the Author Profile page at Harlequin.com.

CAST OF CHARACTERS

Jen Jordan—Single mother who will stop at nothing to find her missing roommate and best friend, Madison Cramer, even when the trouble Madison found comes hunting Jen instead.

Knox Winchester—Jefferson County, Kentucky, deputy sheriff, determined to protect Jen and her six-month-old son, D.J., whatever the cost, while locating and returning her missing roommate safely.

Cruz Winchester—Local private investigator and older brother of Knox Winchester, committed to helping protect Jen and her baby while searching for her missing roommate.

Derek Winchester—Cruz's partner at their PI firm, a cousin by blood and brother by upbringing. Always willing to help his family any way he can.

Blaze Winchester—West Liberty homicide detective, assisting his cousins and brother in the safe return of Madison Cramer.

Madison Cramer—Jen's missing best friend and roommate.

Katie Arnold—Receptionist at the clinic where Madison works, believed to have details about her situation and location.

Chapter One

Jen Jordan adjusted her six-month-old son, D.J., in the baby sling across her chest, as she moved through the Crestwood Kentucky Community Center. Her days as a swim coach had transitioned to evenings as a swim instructor when Dylan Jr. was born, but she didn't miss the coaching, not when she had a perfect cherub-faced little swimmer of her own to care for. She and D.J. had just wrapped another eight-week set of Water Babies lessons, a small mommy-and-me-style class designed to help parents and their up-to-two-years-old children relax and bond. And Jen was ready to celebrate.

Her phone exploded with the pops and dings of waiting messages, texts and notifications as she exited the old stone building, populating with news of everything she'd missed while in the pool and locker room.

She dialed her roommate, Madison, on her way through the lobby. Madison hadn't answered Jen's calls before class, but their shared location-tracking app had suggested she was at the park, a place she often went to think. She supposed Madison had gotten lost in a good book, or an enthralling run, but the sun was setting now, and Madison should be home. With a little luck, she hadn't already eaten, because Jen planned to treat tonight.

"What should we get for dinner?" she asked D.J. as she waited for the call to connect.

D.J. cooed and blew spit bubbles, clearly happy with whatever the adults decided. He'd be as thrilled with tonight's bottle as every one before it. His chubby arms and dimpled fists pumped cheerfully as she tousled his curly brown hair.

Her call to Madison went to voice mail.

Maybe she was in the shower.

Jen unlocked her car and strapped her son safely into his rear-facing car seat, enjoying the warm summer breeze across her cheek and in her still-damp hair. "If Auntie Maddie doesn't answer soon, Mommy's choosing pad Thai," she told him, then dropped a flurry of kisses over his cheeks, nose and forehead until he laughed.

She slipped into the driver's seat and locked the doors, then checked her phone once more. She and Madison had downloaded a tracking app for friends months ago, when Jen was still pregnant and constantly feared something might happen to her or her baby. She'd worried daily that some bizarre, unforeseen tragedy would strike while she was out somewhere alone. The app had made her feel as if, whatever happened, Madison could find her. The heightened paranoia was, no doubt, a side effect of losing her fiancé, Dylan, and Madison's husband, Bob, only months prior. The men had been victims of a roadside bomb shortly after leaving their military base in Afghanistan. Both soldiers had been due home, permanently, this summer. If things had gone differently, Jen and Dylan would've been planning their wedding right now, and Madison would be celebrating her fifth anniversary with Bob. But life had a way of turning everything upside down. Dylan Jr. was proof of that. She hadn't even realized she was pregnant until after the funeral. So she'd spent most of her unexpected pregnancy afraid of when the next tragedy would strike, and certain she couldn't withstand another loss.

Thankfully, Madison had been a good sport about the app, and they'd used it frequently for fun things, like impromptu outings, meals and meetups.

Jen frowned at the phone, then stared through her windshield at the twilight settling over the town. According to the app, Madison was still at the park, but why? Madison was the first person to lecture Jen about the dangers of being out alone after dark, even knowing Jen could take care of herself. She was right, of course, because basic self-defense had its limits. Especially if an attacker was armed, or erratic, and thanks to a new street drug in the community, crime was on the rise.

If Madison was ten years younger, and not grieving the loss of her husband, Jen might've suspected she'd met someone and didn't want to say goodbye. But that wasn't the case, and when Jen returned her gaze to her phone, the little avatar representing Madison disappeared.

She tapped the screen, then closed and reopened the app, but nothing changed. Either Madison had uninstalled the app, or her phone was powered off. Neither seemed reasonable. Though it was possible, Jen supposed, that her friend's phone battery had died.

An odd bolt of intuition and fear stilled her breaths and limbs, then her heart began to race. She dialed Madison again, set the phone in her car's cup holder, then shifted into Drive. The park wasn't far from the community center. She could be there in ten minutes or less, if traffic cooperated.

This time the call went directly to voice mail. As it would if the phone's battery was dead. She blew out a long breath and tried to loosen her grip on the wheel, but it was too late. The possibility Madison was in danger, no matter how unlikely, was more than Jen could stand. She'd relax when she knew her friend was safe, and not a moment sooner.

She raced across town at five miles above the posted speed limit, careful to avoid lanes with turning cars and slow drivers. She redialed Madison at every red light and stop sign along the way. Each with the same result. Voice mail.

Wherever Madison was, if her phone was dead, she still hadn't plugged it in.

Jen hit the turn signal and piloted her little sedan through the park's entrance only eight minutes after leaving work. The lot was empty, the lawns, playgrounds and ball fields devoid of people. Her nerves were strung impossibly tight. She'd told herself not to panic, that the emotions she felt were a result of residual grief and trauma, nothing more. But instinct clawed at her.

No, she told herself. She and Madison didn't live in a war zone. There weren't any roadside bombs or looming enemies. There were museums and parks. Libraries and restaurants. Recent drug-related incidents aside, Crestwood was a great place to live.

She lowered the volume on the radio as she drove through the small rectangular parking area, thankful Madison's car wasn't abandoned in one of the spaces. Another tally in her mental column of reasons *not* to suspect she'd been abducted.

Unless Madison had walked or jogged to the park. If so, it wouldn't have been the first time, even this week.

Jen powered her window down and scanned the silent area, unwilling to park or get out at night with D.J. When no one came into view, she drove on, navigating the long narrow access road to an old carousel where Madison liked to sit and read.

Her senses stayed on high alert as gravel crunched, impossibly loud, beneath her tires. The sliver of cloud-covered moon in a bruised indigo sky did nothing to help her search.

The carousel creaked and rattled with a heavy gust of July wind when she drew near. The attraction was historic and normally busy until ten o'clock on summer weekends, but a stalled restoration project had put an end to that for now. And at the moment, the usually whimsical ride, with its bridled horses and mirrored accents, seemed more like something from a nightmare than a fairy tale. Even the park itself seemed to have taken on a sinister vibe. Funny how something so beautiful by day could seem so entirely foreboding at nightfall.

Jen nudged the gas pedal and concentrated on projecting her voice, without alarming anyone who might be nearby. "Madison?"

The world was eerily silent, filled with the reaching limbs and creeping shadows of ancient leafy trees. An erratic security light flickered and buzzed overhead, raising the fine hairs on the back of her neck and arms to attention. The shape of a dark sedan was barely visible beyond the light, obscured so effectively by shadow she wasn't completely sure what she saw. Who would park back here at this hour and why? Teens making out? Something stolen and abandoned? She swallowed hard and hoped the reason wasn't anything more heinous.

"Madison?" she tried again, feeling the sudden lightning bolt of certainty that something was truly wrong. She strained her eyes against the suffocating night, willing her friend to appear, then dialed her number once more before finally turning the car around. The call, again, went to voice mail.

She idled another moment, accessing the texts and messages she'd missed while in the community center's cement dungeon of a pool and locker room. She'd thought to do so earlier, before Madison's avatar had disappeared and redirected her thoughts. No voice mails. A ton of spam emails. And a single missed text.

Madison: Don't go home. Wait for my call.

The text had been sent nearly two hours ago.

The sharp crack of breaking twigs pulled her attention to the space beyond the carousel, where a figure had stepped into view. For one brief moment, she imagined it was Madison, and in the next she understood it was not. A large dark silhouette moved in her direction, too broad and tall to be her friend.

The long determined strides of the stranger made it clear he was coming for Jen, not simply headed her way. And as he passed beneath the flickering security light, his balaclava became perfectly visible. As did his gun.

She jerked the shifter into Reverse and pressed the gas pedal with purpose, putting space between her car, her baby and the figure.

Her heart cried out for Madison's safety, knowing this couldn't be a coincidence. The app had said Madison was here, and now she was gone, a masked gunman in her place.

He stilled in the flickering light as she piloted her little car away.

Chapter Two

Jefferson County Deputy Sheriff, Knox Winchester, fell onto his desk chair with a low growl. Frustrated, exhausted and hungry, he'd already worked an hour beyond his shift, and thanks to the new street drug, MX-10, which had been wreaking havoc on his town, he still had paperwork to complete.

He glared at his watch, then forced himself to sit taller and get started. The sooner he finished, the sooner he could leave. And a week of vacation awaited him on the other side of the sheriff's department door. He was well beyond due for that break and damn ready.

Knox rolled his shoulders, trying and failing to alleviate the knots of tension in the bunched muscles of his neck and back. He needed to go for a run or hit the gym, anything to shed the weight he'd carried away from his last stop of the day. A death scene more tragic than most, and one that was sure to haunt him the rest of his days.

He dutifully began to write as images of MX-10's

most recent victim returned to him. Today, the casualty had been a young mother of three small children. She was barely twenty, and living in a small run-down apartment, when she'd overdosed. Her sons, a three-, two- and one-year-old, had been left without care for days before a neighbor finally responded to the crying. The older woman found the body and called the sheriff's department.

The home was a wreck. The kids were filthy and hungry. The preschooler had been feeding his siblings peanut butter and water, waiting for Mommy to wake up. It was a wonder the children had survived. Knox couldn't imagine what those few days would do to the oldest boy as he grew. The other two were unlikely to remember the specifics, though Knox suspected the experience would linger somewhere inside them as they aged. And he didn't dare think of what their lives had been like leading up to Mom's final dose.

Knox groaned, angry and heartsick, pushing the images from his mind, demanding himself to finish the job and claim his hard-earned time off.

An hour later, he felt the weight of the burden lift. He stretched onto his feet, finished with the day and his work, then headed into the hallway. He bypassed the door to the gym, only interested in getting home, taking off his uniform and hitting the shower. At twenty-seven and single on a Friday night, he had the wild plans of a man twice his age, and he was utterly eager to get started. Tonight, there would be steak, cooked and enjoyed on his rear deck beneath the stars. Perfectly scored, thanks to the new gas grill he'd splurged on last spring. Nature. Solitude. Steak. A perfect trifecta.

He slung his duffel bag onto one shoulder and took a deep breath as he headed out, feeling the weight of exhaustion on his mood and limbs. He unbuttoned his uniform shirt at the collar and quickened his pace. A moment later, the lobby came into view, and he raised his hand in goodbye to the intake desk, where Deputy Riley spoke to a beautiful but thoroughly upset woman with a baby.

Knox turned away quickly and kept his eyes on the sliver of moonlight outside the glass double doors. People had problems all the time. Even pretty people with babies. And he would be back to help in nine days.

Right now, he was twenty feet from freedom.

"I need to see Knox Winchester," the woman said, pulling Knox up short.

He slowed to take another look at the woman.

Her cheeks were red and tearstained. Her breaths came in frantic bursts.

Her baby kicked merrily from his position in a sling around her torso.

"I'm sorry," Riley replied, sliding his gaze quickly to Knox, then back. "Deputy Winchester's shift ended hours ago, but I can get someone else to help you."

The woman's shoulders sagged and she nodded. "I called emergency dispatch on my way here. I asked them to look for my friend and a man with a gun at Carousel Park. Can you tell me if they found them?"

Riley's brows rose slightly. "There's a man with a gun in the park?"

Knox released a defeated sigh, turned on his heels and headed back across the lobby, away from his vacation. "I can take it from here," he told the other deputy, offering a tired but appreciative smile. Riley had tried to let him escape, but what else could be done now?

And Knox was more than a little intrigued by the idea this woman somehow knew him. Or had at least been instructed to ask for him.

The woman's mouth opened, then closed, clearly stunned to see him, despite the fact she'd requested him by name.

He extended a hand in her direction and their gazes met. "I'm—" The words lodged in his throat as a strange familiarity zinged in his tired mind.

"I know," she said, ignoring his offered hand. "You probably don't remember me."

"I remember you," he said, the words nearly landing on top of hers. The flash of images and emotions that hit next were so intense they might've doubled him over if he wasn't suddenly frozen. The fresh swell of grief stole his breath. Memories of the day they'd met took him right back to the moment. She'd worn a black dress and blank expression. She'd been sullen and silent. He'd wanted to introduce himself and tell her he'd loved Dylan too, but she'd kept vanishing, like a ghost in the crowd. Then he'd stepped outside at Dylan's mother's house during the wake, overwrought when Dylan's dad had broken down in tears. And she'd been there.

Knox had stolen a bottle of whiskey from the makeshift bar near the kitchen, then wandered onto the porch. Jen was sitting on the back steps, staring at nothing and drinking red wine from the bottle. The instant camaraderie had anchored him. And when she'd smiled at something he'd said, he was certain they would get through their loss. If a smile was still possible, on a day like that, then he supposed anything was.

How long ago had that been, exactly? *A year now*, he thought. Maybe a month or two more.

His gaze dropped to the baby, and he recalled her with the wine. Had she been pregnant that day? She'd been sick. He'd had to convince her to eat something when she'd started to look peaked and green. They'd assumed the nausea was a result of the awful day, and alcohol on an empty stomach, but the boy's brown curls and dark round eyes told another story. Jen hadn't gotten pregnant after Dylan's death. That was Dylan's child in her arms.

Dylan Stark had been Knox's bunkmate for two years while he'd finished his time in the US army. Dylan had been fairly new. They'd been like brothers. Then Knox had returned to civilian life and become a deputy. Three years later, Dylan had died senselessly during a routine outing with Bob Cramer in the seat Knox had once occupied.

"It's been a while," he said, controlling his tone and emotion, as well as watching his words. She was clearly spooked, and had said something about a gunman.

She wet her lips, and her eyes glistened with unshed tears. "Fourteen months. This is D.J."

"Dylan Jr.?" he asked, rhetorically, the answer blatantly obvious.

She nodded again, and a tear swiveled over her cheek. "Please help me."

"Of course. Tell me everything." He dropped his duffel, crossed his arms and widened his stance, offering 100 percent of his attention.

Her thin fingers curled protectively around the baby tucked against her chest. "There was a man with a gun at the park. I called emergency services on my way here because my roommate isn't answering her phone, and according to an app we share, she was at the carousel only a few minutes before I saw him. Two hours before that, she sent me a text, telling me not to go home, but I didn't get that message until I'd seen the gunman."

"Any signs of her at the park?" he asked.

"No."

Knox looked to Riley, who returned the desk phone's handset to its receiver. "Any word?"

"I just spoke to Deputy Lee," Riley said. "They

swept the park near the carousel. No signs of a gunman or the woman."

"Thanks," Knox said. He tipped his head toward
the long hallway he'd just walked. Then led Jen to
his desk and offered her a bottle of water. He listened
carefully as she set out the facts for him. Bob's wife,
Madison, was her missing roommate. Knox hadn't
known Bob, but his friendship with Dylan spoke volumes about his character. Dylan had had high expec-
tations and inflexible moral standards for himself and
the people around him.

"All right," he said, as comfortingly as he could
manage, after her official report was made. "How
about I follow you home. We'll see if it looks like
anyone's been there and decide what to do next."

Jen's eyes were distant as she stroked her baby's
chubby arm and dimpled hand. When she dragged
her attention back to him, resolve had formed there.
"Okay."

Twenty minutes later, Knox parked his truck beside Jen's sedan outside a row of newly developed
apartments a few blocks from downtown. There
hadn't been any signs of Madison or a shooter at the
park, and Knox could only hope that was good news.
Perhaps the man with a gun had been a random criminal looking for an easy target this time of evening,
and Madison's phone had simply died. Maybe the
man hadn't had a gun at all. It was dark, and Jen had
been frightened when she saw him. Maybe the fear

and shadows had given a completely normal situation an ominous tilt.

He re-buttoned his uniform shirt and abandoned his dreams of relaxation and steak, then put his deputy sheriff hat back on, figuratively and literally. "Here we go," he told himself, climbing out of his truck. Hopefully, Madison was in better shape than the last woman whose home he'd visited.

He rounded the hood in Jen's direction, shoulders back and jaw set. "Which one is yours?"

Jen's cheeks were ruddy once more as she locked her car and met him on the sidewalk with her son. "Two A."

Knox led the way, easily navigating the unfamiliar building. He stopped several feet before their destination, when her apartment came into view. The door was partially open, and a visible mess waited inside.

Chapter Three

Jen's breath caught. Her heart raced and ears rang. The apartment door was open, and from what she could see, hiding behind Knox in the hallway, her home had been ransacked. Thoughts of the masked gunman collided with memories of Madison's text. Panic twisted in her core as she imagined what might've happened inside. An endless stream of ugly and terrifying possibilities weakened her knees.

Knox bent his elbow and raised one fist, silently indicating she should stay where she was. Then he removed the gun from his holster and entered her apartment with the stealth and confidence of a man who'd done this before.

Jen bounced gently, rocking her son and attempting to burn off the energy produced by misplaced adrenaline. She counted silently to measure the passage of time, and sent up endless, fervent pleas that Madison was inside. Safe and alive.

The hope seemed almost childish. Definitely illogical and unreasonable. If Madison were inside, she would've called the sheriff's department herself when an intruder came to the door. If she were okay, the door wouldn't be standing partly open. And if she were home, why had the app said she was at the park?

Had the home already been ransacked when Madison sent the text in warning? Or did she have a reason to suspect it might be?

Jen shook the thought away. How could anyone know in advance their home would be broken into? And if she'd known, why hadn't she called the sheriff's department?

Distant shuffling sounds turned her attention back to the open door. Knox had been inside too long, and she didn't want to be alone in the hallway anymore. She stepped carefully forward, crossing the threshold, prepared to deal with whatever awaited on the other side.

From her new position, she could see across the expanse of her open-concept home. A change from carpet to tile separated the dinette from the living room. Beyond that, an island delineated the dinette from the kitchen. Jen's old desk stood against one wall in the living room and acted as a communal work space. Jen had moved her desk months ago to make room for D.J.'s crib. Madison had another small desk in her room. A hall along the wall with the front door led to the bedrooms and a shared bath.

Knox's voice carried to her ears, speaking quickly on what seemed to be a phone call, presumably to the sheriff's department.

D.J. fussed, and her arms curled tenderly over him. She kissed his head and whispered sweetly, attempting to mask the anxiety and fear pouring off her.

Knox appeared in the hall outside her bedroom a moment later, missing a beat before continuing back to her side. "You aren't where I left you," he said, his gun safely back in its holster.

Jen's shoulders crept upward, towed by tension. "Any signs of Madison?"

"No, but someone's clearly been here."

Around her, the apartment's condition began to take focus. Papers from her desk were scattered over the floor, but her new monitor was still in place. The couch had been taken apart, cushions tossed, along with her grandmother's afghan, yet the television remained. Her kitchen drawers and cabinets stood open. The pantry contents had been thoroughly toppled, but Madison's phone dock, portable speaker and wireless earbuds were untouched on the countertop. "I don't think anything's missing," she said, the words creaking from her throat.

Nothing, except Madison.

"There aren't any signs of forced entry, and it doesn't seem like a robbery," he agreed, eyes skimming the scene. "No distinctive signs of a struggle," he said, setting broad palms over narrow hips. "My best guess is that someone was looking for something."

"What could anyone possibly want from us?" She nearly laughed at the thought. Everything she and

Madison had of value was either still in sight or at the bank, not that either of their accounts were especially impressive. "Could the intruder have been looking for cash or credit cards?"

"Maybe," Knox said, turning sharp green eyes back on her. "I called the station. I'm officially on vacation, so other deputies will make the report and handle the crime scene. I won't leave unless you ask me. Meanwhile, I'd like to talk to your neighbors, see if anyone saw or heard anything."

D.J. squirmed against Jen's chest, and she willed herself to remain calm.

"Okay." She moved to the kitchen and sat at the small table, unloading the bottle and formula from D.J.'s diaper bag. It was time to feed her baby, but she didn't dare touch anything unnecessarily until she was told it wouldn't interfere with whatever the deputies needed to do. If there was a clue in the apartment that would lead them to Madison's location, she wanted to be sure Knox or the other deputies would find it.

He moved toward the door. "Will you be okay here, if I step out for a few?"

She nodded. "I'll try calling her phone again."

"Good." He looked down the hall in each direction, then back to Jen. "Do you have a building manager? Someone who overlooks the property?"

She poured premeasured formula into a bottle already filled with water, then gave D.J.'s next meal a shake. "Mrs. Hancock is on our floor," she said, forcing her tone to sound stronger than she felt. "Apartment 2K at the end of the hall."

Knox walked out, pulling the door shut behind him, and her shoulders slumped in response.

She lifted D.J. from the sling and kissed his head, then rested him in the crook of her arm and offered the bottle. His dark brows furrowed as he watched her, sensing her tension, even as he eagerly accepted the meal. "It's okay," she whispered, more to herself than him. "Aunt Maddie will be okay."

Jen needed that to be true more than she'd needed anything in a long time. Madison had been through too much already. It wasn't fair for her to have to endure this too. Whatever this was.

She set her phone on the table and dialed her friend once more.

Voice mail.

Knox returned a few moments later, speaking her name as he knocked, probably so she wouldn't jump out of her skin. She rose on wooden legs to let him in.

"No one answered at the manager's place," he said, bypassing a traditional, though wholly unnecessary, greeting. "A set of deputies are pulling into the parking lot now." He glanced at his phone, then cast his attention to the steps. "I'll brief them before bringing them inside."

Jen carried D.J. back to the kitchen, unsure what to say or how to feel about more deputies in her apartment, then reclaimed her seat.

Knox stood in the open doorway, stealing curious looks in her direction while she stared unapologetically back.

He was tall and lean. His posture screamed authority, and a muscle in his jaw clenched and released repeatedly, betraying his exterior calm. She'd only met Knox twice, but it was easy to see he was made for the uniform and not the other way around. Even years after leaving the military, the soldier he'd been was visible just below the surface. In the way he moved. The way he carried himself. And the almost-over-the-top composure.

She wondered if the evident self-control was present in everything he did, on and off the clock. Then she hated herself for the shockingly inappropriate thought.

Clearly, unlike Knox, Jen was not built to sustain emotional pressure. She was already starting to crack.

He widened his stance and joined his hands behind his back. The soldier pressed himself against the surface once more.

Jen admired the look. There was something profound about the men and women who pledged their lives to the protection of others. She respected them in ways she could never quite articulate. Until she'd become a mother, it had been hard to understand how one person could put themselves in harm's way for another, because she'd never felt the need to protect anyone at all costs like that. It was easier now, knowing there weren't limits to what she would do for D.J. Still, she wasn't as selfless when it came to the public at large. Because if she let something happen to her, who would care for her baby? And ultimately, D.J.'s safety was all that truly mattered.

The soft sounds of footfalls on carpet reached her ears, and Knox lifted his chin.

A man and woman wearing uniforms identical to Knox's appeared. The trio spoke quietly before Knox led them inside.

"This is Jen Jordan and her son, D.J.," he told the newcomers. "Jen, this is Deputy Van and Deputy Wence. They're going to take over from here."

The pair nodded, then went to work. The woman, Deputy Wence, crouched and unpacked a duffel with the sheriff's department logo, apparently preparing to dust the front door for fingerprints. The man, Deputy Van, headed down the hall.

Knox joined Jen and D.J. in the kitchen. "Can I get you a glass of water?"

Her instinct was to decline. Manners dictated that she should be serving him. He was the guest, which made her the host. Except that explanation for their current roles didn't work. Knox wasn't a guest, not in the traditional sense, and it didn't matter anyway, because when she opened her mouth, the words didn't come.

The situation was too surreal to be true.

Knox checked the refrigerator, then used the pitcher he found there to fill a glass with cold water. He set it on the table, then took a beat to close all the open cupboards. "Why don't we make a list of

Madison's local friends and family while the other deputies work," he suggested. "Places she liked to frequent. Coworkers she spent time with. And anyone else she might've been in touch with this afternoon or evening."

"Thank you," Jen said, lifting the glass. She was suddenly parched at the sight of it and drank deeply.

The list he wanted would be simple and short.

"Madison's family lives in Missouri," she said. "She moved here about nine months ago, when my pregnancy became high-risk. Everything is still new to her. She texts to ask for directions to things that are only a few blocks away. It doesn't make any sense that she would be targeted by someone."

Deputy Wence finished dusting for prints, then removed a camera from her black supply bag and began photographing the mess. When she moved on from the living room, Knox began to reassemble the couch.

"Have you noticed anything different about Madison lately?" he asked. "Was she jumpy? Withdrawn?"

"Not really." Jen shifted D.J. against her chest, rubbing his back gently after setting his drained bottle aside. She tried to remember the last conversation she'd had with her roommate, but the days had gone fuzzy since she'd returned to work at the community center. After twelve weeks off with a newborn, adjusting to any sort of schedule D.J. didn't personally set was tough. And Jen often taught evening classes, while Madison worked days. "I'm not sure," she amended. "Our schedules don't always line up."

Knox crouched to collect the papers scattered on the floor, then sifted through them as he made a tidy pile. "Was she seeing anyone?"

A humorless laugh bubbled up from Jen's chest. "Definitely not."

"You sure? Dating seems like a great way to make connections in a new town."

"I'm positive," she said. And if Knox knew Madison at all, he'd have understood how absurd the concept actually was. "Madison is still grieving Bob's death."

Knox stood, then straightened the contents of her desk before making his way through the living room, cleaning as he went. When he finished there, he returned to the kitchen. "I see."

He righted fallen formula cans and prepackaged staples in the pantry. "This is a pretty serious mess," he said. "Given Madison's text, warning you not to come home, it's safe to say the intrusion wasn't random." He turned to face her, resting his backside against the countertop. "Something is going on here. We just have to figure out what that is. She goes off-grid on the night you see a man with a gun, at the place she was last known to be. Then the apartment you share with her is ransacked on the same night. You say she doesn't date or know anyone other than you in Crestwood, so you're going to have to dig deep and come up with something we can use to find her."

"I don't know anything," Jen said, the words erupting with a frustrated snap.

Knox lowered himself onto the seat across from her, scanning her features with practiced eyes. Likely seeing the barely tamped panic she didn't want to show. "Let's try something else. Why don't you tell me about Madison? Start anywhere you'd like."

"She and Bob were married five years," Jen said, the thought popping instantly into mind. "They were from the same small town in Missouri. They practically grew up together, and they had the perfect relationship. When I first met her, I was sure she was the happiest person I'd ever known. We stayed in touch, online and by phone, for about two years before…"

The muscle in Knox's jaw tightened and released again. "How's she been since Bob's death?"

"Not the same." The weight of the words settled over her, and she took a long beat before pressing on. Jen had never told anyone about the impact Bob's death had had on Madison. And despite all that was happening, it felt a little like betrayal to say it now.

Knox waited. Serious eyes searching, and his disposition as patient as ever.

Jen finished the glass of water, then attempted to breathe in his enviable calm. "I think part of Madison died with Bob that day. I didn't realize until weeks later. I'd been so busy getting through my loss, then the unexpected news that D.J. was on the way, that I hadn't called. By the time I realized she wasn't posting on her social media and hadn't emailed or texted me since the funerals, the depression had already pulled her under. She lost a lot of weight, wasn't eating, couldn't get out of bed or go to work. It was bad. I thought I might lose her too, and I demanded she not do that to me. When I told her my pregnancy was flagged as high-risk, that I was scared and unsure how I was supposed to get through it on my own, she put her house on the market and moved to Crestwood. She's been coming back to herself here. A little bit, day by day. It was as if she completely shifted her energy from absorbing the overwhelming grief to being whatever D.J. and I needed. When my maternity leave ended, and it was time for me to go back to work, she did too."

"But your work schedules are different," Knox said, repeating the fact Jen had offered earlier. "So, it's possible she got a new friend or found a hobby she hadn't told you about yet."

"I guess," Jen admitted, "but that would've had to be recent. I'm sure I would've noticed otherwise, and Madison is an excellent judge of character. She has a sixth sense about people. She'd never intentionally entangle herself with someone capable of this." She dragged her gaze over the recently destroyed apartment.

Knox rested his clasped hands on the table between them. "Is it possible she was slipping back into depression and just hadn't told you? Or can you think of anything else that would explain why she stopped answering her phone?"

Jen searched her memories for some kind of

warning signs that Madison's life had taken a negative turn. Had she been so sleep-deprived and baby-obsessed that she hadn't noticed? Madison had spent more time in her room than usual, but Jen assumed adjusting to full-time work after nearly a year off was exhausting. Plus, Madison worked days. She went to bed early so she could get up early. She still helped with D.J. anytime Jen needed.

But what if something had been wrong, and Jen had missed it?

"Sometimes people who've been through a major loss like hers will act out," Knox said. "They can behave recklessly, in rebellion to the fact life is short and incredibly fragile. And people who struggle with depression often find it a vicious cycle, rarely letting go for very long."

Jen stared, suddenly seeing Knox for the deputy sheriff he was, and not simply the friend she'd met at Dylan's funeral, then run to for help. Knox was going through the motions, treating Madison like any other missing person and asking a standard list of canned questions. Too many of which implied Madison might've had something to do with whatever was going on.

Jen leaned forward, feathers thoroughly ruffled as she cuddled D.J. against her. "Madison is in trouble," she bit out. "She's a victim. And we need to help her. She didn't suddenly break bad and get involved with criminals."

Deputy Wence returned, interrupting Jen's rant

and drawing Knox's attention. She presented her hand, a plastic baggie of white pills caught between two fingertips. "This was inside the bathroom cabinet, taped to the underside of the sink."

Chapter Four

Knox slid a measured gaze from the pills in Deputy Wence's hand to Jen, willing himself to remain composed, while recognizing the little white devils for what they were. MX-10. "Are those yours?" he asked Jen, gently scanning her stunned face.

"No." The word was breathless, and her eyes wide. "I don't understand." She dragged her attention, reluctantly, from the baggie to Knox.

He lifted a hand, dismissing the other deputy, who easily walked away, taking the evidence with her. "If the drugs aren't yours..." he said, leaving the sentence unfinished for a long beat "...there's only one other person they can belong to."

"Madison doesn't do drugs," she said. "Maybe the pills were left behind by the previous tenant."

Knox shook his head as she spoke, and her expression turned to a frown. "I don't think so."

"Why not?" she asked. "How can you possibly know for sure? It's not as if I've ever checked underneath my sink's basin for contraband. That bag might've been there for years."

"It hasn't," Knox said confidently. "In fact, I doubt it's been there more than a few weeks. A month or two at the very most, and even that's highly unlikely."

Jen's eyes narrowed in frustration and disbelief. "And I suppose you can be sure of all that after one fleeting look at a baggie of random pills, from two feet away? Is that some kind of special gift? Like the man who can guess my weight at the fair?"

Knox eyeballed her, almost certain she weighed about one hundred and fifty pounds, but didn't dare test his skill. He'd learned long ago never to mention a woman's weight, because no matter what the number truly was, she wasn't happy with it. "They weren't random," he said. "And yes, I can identify MX-10 from much farther away. I've seen enough of it in the last month to make me an expert in everything except its personal use and the location of manufacturing. I have no intention to ever gain firsthand experience about the former, and I would give anything for details on the latter," he fumed, the sight of the drug in Jen's home raising his hackles. He hated that MX-10 had reached her world, even peripherally. "That trash is killing this city, and it's spreading to other towns within my county and jurisdiction. Surely, you've seen the news."

Jen's expression turned distant, and he thought she might be recalling one of the many recent reports about a spike in local crime and overdoses related to this new street drug. "I have," she said. "But that doesn't make any sense. Madison wouldn't do drugs," she reaffirmed. "And even if she did, which she wouldn't, I know she'd never bring them into our home. Not with D.J. here."

"Look," he said, carefully tucking his remaining ruffled feathers out of view. "I've got hidden MX-10 at the apartment of a missing woman who's new to town, has a history of depression and has recently disappeared. The facts are painting a different story than you want to hear, and I'm sure that's tough, but we'll figure it out."

She covered her mouth with one hand, astonished and confused.

"MX-10 reached our county about six weeks ago," Knox said. "How long have you been in this apartment?"

Jen looked at the baby in her arms. "A year. Madison's been here nine months."

"Maybe we can make a list of anyone who's visited in the past month or two," he suggested.

Her chest rose and fell in slow measured breaths. "We don't get company."

"Never?" he asked, trying to sound as disbelieving as he felt. He was lucky to go twenty-four hours without a visit from his auntie, brother or at least one cousin.

"I'm in mommy-survival mode right now," she said. "I work and raise D.J. There isn't much time for anything else. Madison is the same. She works and helps me. It's just us here."

Knox pushed back on his chair, stretching his legs beneath the table, and weighing the possibility Jen had been blind to her roommate's troubles. It seemed unlikely. In fact, Jen seemed like the kind of person who missed very little, though she might not always comment.

Deputies Van and Wence returned to the kitchen, having apparently finished their work. They paused at the door to collect the duffels and pack their equipment.

Knox excused himself and went to see them out.

The deputies promised to keep him in the loop as Madison's case unfolded, and he locked the door behind them with a bit of relief.

Jen watched him from her seat at the table. The lost look in her eyes tugged at something deep in his core.

"Have you eaten?" he asked, clasping his palms, then giving them a little rub for friction. "I've officially missed dinner, and it seems like some brain food might help us figure out what we're missing."

She rolled her glossy eyes up to meet his gaze, then blinked back a round of unshed tears. "I could eat."

"Good." He rocked back on his heels and worked up his best smile. "How about I order us something good, then stick around and help with the rest of this cleanup?"

A little voice in his mind begged her to agree. Another piece of him worried he wanted an affirmative answer for all the wrong reasons. His attraction to Jen was natural. She was strong, beautiful and kind. And Knox was only human. But she'd been in love with his best friend once. She'd be a married woman today had things turned out differently.

She nodded, and for a fleeting moment, he thought she was agreeing with his train of thought. That he shouldn't be thinking about the ways he wanted to comfort her. *A warm embrace. A caress of her cheek.* When her face flushed suddenly, he realized he'd been staring.

"How about burgers?" she asked, breaking the awkward silence and turning to search through a scattered pile of take-out menus on the island. "Do you like The Bistro?"

"Yep." Knox took her order, then made the call, and thirty minutes later, he and Jen sat at her table for dinner.

D.J. was fast asleep in his crib, and the apartment was silent and still.

They'd cleaned while they'd waited for the meal to arrive, vacuuming carpets and wiping surfaces. Jen had understandably seemed to put her heart and soul into the efforts. Likely attempting to release the pent-up anxiety while erasing all traces of the intruder from her home.

She ferried two fresh glasses of water to the table, while Knox unpacked their meals.

She'd swept her straight brown hair into a messy knot at the top of her head, and a number of errant tendrils had worked their way loose.

He tracked the strands with his gaze as they fluttered against the curve of her neck when she took the seat across from him.

"Thank you," she said softly, looking as exhausted as she likely felt.

His heart went out to her yet again. She'd been through so much already. Did she have to experience the disappearance of her friend too?

"I've been hanging around here all evening," he said, unwrapping his burger and arranging his fries on the open paper. "The least I can do is buy you dinner."

She gave a soft laugh, then lifted the glass of iced water to her lips. "I'm glad you're here," she said, setting the glass aside after a long careful sip. "But I'm sorry I ruined your vacation."

Knox quirked his brow. How had she remembered Riley mentioning that at the sheriff's department? She'd been so upset at the time, Knox wouldn't have blamed her if the entire encounter had been a blur.

"I know you don't have to be here. It means a lot to me that you are. You certainly didn't have to help me clean the house or buy me dinner."

He wiped the corners of his mouth with a paper napkin and smiled. "I think my auntie would disagree. What kind of person would leave you here alone, upset and with a mess?" His gaze traveled to the door, recalling the most important step that had yet to be taken. "I'm going to make sure your building manager has the locks changed tomorrow. How do you feel about an overnight guest until then? I'd sleep on the couch, of course. Just in case whoever was here earlier gets any ideas about coming back."

Jen's ivory skin paled, and she set her burger aside. "You would do that?"

"I'd like to, yeah," he said. "If you'll have me."

A strange pink hue rose over her cheeks, and she lowered her eyes to the food before her. "Okay."

They ate for several more moments in companionable, if oddly charged, silence. Eventually, Knox decided to unpack the elephant in the room.

"I can't believe you live this close and I didn't know," he said. "I should've come by to check on you at some point." She'd been grieving, alone and pregnant. Madison had sold her home and moved to another state to be with her, but Knox had never even considered looking her up.

"We only met once," she said. "You didn't have any reason to show up."

"True, but I knew you were hurting," he said.

Jen's lips lifted into a gentle smile. "So were you. For what it's worth, I never thought about looking you up to see if you were okay."

Knox's throat tightened uncomfortably, and he took a minute to wipe his mouth and breathe. The unpredictable waves of grief had an uncanny way of always catching him off guard. "He was my best friend."

"He was my fiancé," she said. "We both loved him, but that didn't make you any more responsible for me than I was for you. I'm just glad you're here now. It's nice to have a friend who knows about these things." She lifted another fry, then waved it between them, as if to indicate the previous break-in and everything that went along with it. "I don't know what I'd do if you weren't here."

Knox accepted her words, knowing she'd have been just fine without him tonight, the way she had been for the past year. She'd proven herself smart and strong. The app she and Madison shared was a sensible move for two young single women. Remaining calm enough to call emergency services, while heading to the police department, after facing an armed man, was levelheaded and brave. Jen had been poised and patient at every turn, and a misplaced bubble of pride rose in him.

She watched him as she helped herself to another fry. "Tell me about the pills the deputy found," she said. "Help me understand the possible reasons they were hidden here and what could be happening."

He considered her questions, and all the possible answers, none of which she would like.

When he didn't answer quickly, she set the uneaten fry aside and leaned forward, eyes flashing with barely tamped emotion. "I don't know how to sit here and be helpless. Not when Madison is out there in trouble."

"You aren't just sitting here," he said, the contradiction coming easily. "You've done all you can do, and because of that, authorities are looking for your friend far sooner than they would've been otherwise. You were able to track her and report the presence of a shooter. Those are things that will help us locate Madison. Beyond all that, you're protecting and caring for your son. There's no more important job."

Jen slumped in her chair, but nodded.

"To answer your earlier questions," he added, "I can only speculate about what's happening and the pills' involvement. I've seen more MX-10 in the past few weeks than any other drug in my years on the force combined. Our community is flooded with it, and it's deadly. I have no idea why people are still buying and taking it. It's like Russian roulette." He scrubbed a hand over his hair, then clutched the back of his neck, pushing images of a young deceased mother and her small orphaned children from his mind. "A missing person hiding an addictive substance usually adds up to a user who's strung out. Normally, I'd say the person in question is high and her phone is dead. That she'll be home when she comes back down. The overturned apartment makes me think she could be in debt to her dealer, and is being punished or pursued for that."

"Madison wouldn't use drugs," Jen said, repeating her earlier opinion. "What does all this mean to you, if she isn't an addict?"

Knox offered a noncommittal shake of his head. He didn't know Madison, but the facts he had didn't make her look good.

"Do you think it's possible the gunman wasn't at the park for her?" Jen asked. "Could the timing of all this be coincidence?"

He released a long slow breath, hating the plea in her expression. Jen needed hope, but she was asking for truth, and he couldn't give her both. "I don't believe in coincidence, but anything is possible."

She chewed her lip, considering his words. "Do you think we'll find her?" she asked.

"Yes." He sat straighter, glad to offer at least that bit of good news. "Typically, a person identified this quickly as missing will turn up."

As time went on, however, Madison's odds would change for the worse.

"Do you think she's okay?" Jen asked. "Wherever she is?"

"I suppose that depends on what's going on," he said, avoiding the hard truth Jen didn't need right now. Whether Madison had been abducted or was just on the run, she was anything but okay. "It will help if she's in the right headspace, quick-witted and resourceful."

Jen's blue eyes widened, and an expression of hope brightened her face. "Madison is a survivor, and she's very smart."

Knox hated to disagree, but if Madison was using, or involved with MX-10 in any capacity, she was definitely not smart, and he could only hope she was a survivor.

Chapter Five

Jen awoke to the first determined shafts of sunlight through her bedroom curtain. She'd barely slept, and the light was all it had taken to rouse her once more. The sounds and scents of her quietly chugging coffee maker quickened her heart. The previous day and night rushed back to her like a slap, removing the haze of her fitful sleep.

Madison was missing.

And Knox Winchester had slept over.

The thoughts drove her upward in bed. She peeked at her still-sleeping baby, snuggled in the crib a few feet away, then released a grateful sigh. She needed the extra moment to compose herself before diving into mommy mode.

Her cheeks and core heated at the memories of her unexpected and troublesome dreams. She'd fallen asleep afraid for her friend's safety and thankful for Knox's presence. The reassurance he'd offered, and natural way he'd interacted with her and D.J., had clearly confused her exhausted mind, inciting illicit fantasies. Knox was exactly the kind of man she'd always been drawn to, and his unreasonable good looks only fueled the nonsensical fire she'd felt since setting eyes on him at the sheriff's department.

Her dream had begun as a nightmare. She'd been searching the dark park for Madison alone. The gunman had found her, but Knox had saved her. He'd comforted her, hugged her. Then he'd lowered his mouth to taste her lips. The embrace had felt so real, the kiss so sensual, she'd urged him desperately on. She'd woken in a sweat, excited and ashamed. Madison was missing, but her mind was on kissing Knox instead?

Clearly, the situation was more than she could handle, and her brain had gone on the fritz.

She raked a hand through her ratty hair, and swung her feet over the bed's edge, shaking the remaining dirty thoughts from her mind. A large mug of the brewing coffee would put her back in the right headspace. Finding Madison was all that mattered right now.

She grabbed her phone from the nightstand and checked for missed messages. As she'd feared, Madison hadn't reached out.

D.J.'s eyes opened, and Jen sighed. Her moment of solitude had passed, but it was impossible to begrudge the time she now got to spend with her baby. He yawned and stretched chubby, dimpled arms over his head, flashing her a wide gummy smile.

Her heart gave a heavy kick, and she went to him

instantly, feeling the smile split her face in the process. "Well, hello, handsome," she said, lifting him into her arms. "Mommy missed you while you were sleeping. Did you have nice dreams?" She snuggled him close and pressed soft kisses against his warm cheeks and soft downy hair.

D.J. giggled in response.

"How about a fresh diaper and a little breakfast?" she suggested.

Jen changed him quickly, then dressed him in black denim overalls and a white T-shirt with red stars. She tugged matching socks onto his tiny feet and smiled. "So perfect."

He made a cranky face, and she gathered him to her chest once more. Time to make good on her promise of food.

She looked longingly at the blue hoodie crumpled on her floor, considering how fast she could slip it over her tank top and sleep shorts. Putting D.J. down to get the job done seemed unwise as he squirmed in her grip, and she decided it was best to feed him before making any additional delays.

Knox came into view a moment later, leaning casually against her open pantry, a steaming mug in his hand.

The dream she'd just pushed from her mind returned instantly to steal her breath. The strength of his imagined embrace and tenderness of his perfect touch sent a fog of lust and longing across her tired mind.

"Hey," she said, slipping past him to grab the baby formula.

"Good morning," he returned.

His voice was low and rough with fatigue. She might've even been the first person he'd spoken to this morning, and the intimacy in that possibility made her stomach flutter.

"I hope you were able to get a little sleep," she said, focusing tightly on the preparation of D.J.'s bottle. "I can't imagine you were very comfortable." The living room furniture was old and worn. And Knox was at least a foot longer than the couch.

He smiled warmly at D.J., then dragged his cool green eyes back to her. "I did just fine. I hope I didn't wake you."

"Not at all," she said. "I had trouble staying asleep, and this guy likes to rise with the sun." She kissed her son once more, then put the restless night behind her. It was a new day, and that meant a new chance to find her friend. "Have you gotten any news?" she asked, tipping the bottle to her baby's mouth and leaning him back in her arms. "Something about Madison or the gunman? Fingerprints on my door?"

"Not yet," Knox said. He sipped gingerly from his cup, then cast his attention back to the open pantry.

"Hungry?" she asked, wondering if food would make him more agreeable to the set of requests circling in her mind. "I can make something if you want."

Knox shook his head. "I was thinking about making French toast. If you don't mind loaning me your kitchen."

She nearly laughed. Would a stressed-out, sleep-deprived mom mind if a handsome, single lawman made her breakfast? "Knock yourself out," she said. She was tired, not crazy.

He went to work, and she wondered if there was anything he didn't do. He'd appeared as comfortable with a rag and cleanser last night as he did with his badge and gun.

Her heart swelled in appreciation as she moved D.J. to his high chair, then went to pour a mug of coffee. "Did you go home last night?" she asked, realizing he'd somehow managed to change his clothes. "Or do you travel with a change of clothes?"

As much as she'd liked him in his uniform, she could certainly appreciate the view before her as well. A heather-gray T-shirt clung to his chest and biceps, showcasing the lean planes and muscles. Dark wash jeans hugged his narrow hips. He was barefoot in her kitchen, cooking. And she was pretty sure this was how most of her fantasies began. Though the man in her dreams hadn't had a name or face in more than a year, until last night.

Knox arranged ingredients on her countertop, glancing briefly at his clothes. "I keep a go bag in the truck. I'm out overnight unexpectedly more often than you'd think."

She rolled her eyes and sipped from her cup.

"On business," he said, cracking an egg into a bowl. A moment later he added, "Mostly."

Jen shook her head, but managed to keep her thoughts on that topic to herself.

"Vanilla?" he asked, brows raised. "Cinnamon?"

She fished the extract and powder from her baking cabinet, then set both beside his bowl. The caffeine had taken hold, and she was eager to make her request before she chickened out. "I've been thinking," she said, pulling his gaze to hers. "Since there hasn't been any news on Madison, maybe we should come up with a plan."

"A plan?" he echoed, beating the eggs with a fork. "I'm going to need more information."

"Well, you're a cop with time off," she said. "I thought we could work together to figure out what happened to Madison. For starters, we can try to use the app to retrace her steps and figure out what she was up to when things went south."

D.J. began to fuss, empty bottle discarded, and she went to him.

Knox didn't speak, so she continued, "The way I see it, the more people who work this case, the more likely we are to find her," she said. "And I know time is everything. The longer she's gone, the harder it will be to locate her, and the more likely she'll be significantly hurt, or worse, when we do." Jen swallowed the sudden painful lump in her throat, determined to be useful instead of idle. "I'm off work for the weekend, and you're on vacation. We can help."

Knox dropped the first slice of egg-dipped bread onto the heated skillet with a disbelieving laugh. "I had something similar to talk to you about," he said.

She grinned. "Go on."

Knox glanced at her, looking suddenly cautious. "I think you should take D.J. to stay with family or friends for a few days. At least until we figure out what's going on with Madison and the MX-10. That drug isn't something to mess around with, and neither are the people who deal it. We don't even know who the suppliers are, though I've been working on that for months." Frustration raced over his expression, quickly tamped, then replaced with compassion. "There are too many unknowns, and everything that is known spells danger. I appreciate your willingness to help, but you'll both be safer somewhere else." He emphasized the word *both* and tipped his head toward the baby in her arms.

Jen frowned and her stomach knotted. She didn't have friends or family to hide out with. Surely, she'd told him that. It seemed obvious, given that he knew Madison had moved to a new state to help her.

When she didn't respond, Knox pressed on. "Before you argue, remember a gunman saw your car at the park last night, and probably got a good look at you as well. Plus, whoever broke in here would've seen your photos. The intruder had access to personal details while they snooped around. Your place of employment and stores you frequent based on shopping bags, pay stubs and bills. The calendar on your desk tracks your work schedule. It's not safe to stay."

Jen took a seat at the table, hugging her son more tightly and feeling the cutting thread of fear wind painfully in her core. "We don't have anywhere to go," she said, her mouth and throat suddenly dry. "My folks are halfway across the country, and I don't have friends to stay with. I'm not that close to anyone, and bringing a baby is a huge request. Not to mention you think I might be the next target of a gunman. Who can I ask to take us in with that kind of danger in tow?"

"You can fly to your parents," he said. "I'm sure they'd be glad to see you."

She shook her head. "I don't have the money for that, and I won't ask them for it. They kept me financially afloat when I was on bed rest and too stubborn to move to Florida so they could care for me. Plus, my dad isn't well, and I feel as if I've been a source of added stress to them for a year already. It's just complicated."

Knox frowned, the confusion of a man who'd probably never been a burden to anyone visible on his brow.

"Besides," she said, squaring her shoulders, "I want to be here when Madison is found, and I think I can help that process along."

Knox transferred two pieces of French toast to a plate, then delivered them to her at the table, along with a fork, napkin and syrup. He gave her a close inspection before returning to the stove. "You're alone in town?"

"Not alone," she said, kissing D.J. "But yeah."

Knox carried a second plate to the table, then took the seat across from her, digging immediately into his meal. "Do you have somewhere you can spend a day safely? I can come back tonight, if you want." He paused to look at her, then continued cutting his breakfast with a knife and fork. "I'd like to take a look at the carousel. Things might look different by the light of day, and when a car was dispatched last night, the deputy was searching for a gunman, or Madison. They could've missed something."

"Like what?" she asked, a number of awful possibilities rising to the forefront of her mind.

"I'm not sure without looking," he admitted. "That area has a small homeless population, and I typically swing by the park with food and drinks every weekend. Today, I thought I could ask a few questions, see if anyone noticed anything out of the ordinary last night."

She mentally added genuine kindness to her knowledge about Knox. His generosity and selflessness extended beyond what she'd ever imagined. He cared about more than upholding the law and protecting people in danger. Knox cared about his community. All of them, not just the taxpayers. And she warmed impossibly further to him.

"After the park, I thought I'd stop at her place of employment, see if anyone there knows anything about what she's been up to the last few days or weeks. Meanwhile, tech support is trying to locate Madison's phone," Knox added. "If the device is powered on at any point, they'll find it."

"I can go with you," Jen said, setting her fork atop an empty plate. "I helped her find this job as a medical records clerk, and I tagged along for the interview. D.J. and I waited in a café across the street. We can do that today, if you want. We won't be any trouble, and I'd rather stay with you."

Knox sipped his water, considering her. His gaze dropped to her plate. "Can I make you a little more?"

"I'm trying to lose the baby weight, not put it back on." She grinned. "But breakfast was delicious. Thank you."

Knox furrowed his brow once more. "It's none of my business, but for what it's worth, I don't see the weight you think there is to lose."

She rolled her eyes, unwilling to unleash those particular frustrations on him. She really was trying to get back into her old jeans, but so far her body had resisted the efforts. She'd gained forty-five pounds, and only thirty had come off. The remainder had reshaped her body in ways her old wardrobe wasn't prepared to handle. Now, even her formerly most comfortable clothes clung to an abundance of curves. She didn't always hate the look, but it was one more thing in a long line of circumstances she couldn't control. And lack of control was something she despised.

Knox rose with his plate, then added hers to it.

"You'd be welcome at my aunt and uncle's home in West Liberty. My uncle Hank is former military, and carried a badge for twenty years. His property is secure, and he's trained to protect you, not that there's any reason to think it would come to that. I can take you anywhere you want, but I can't take you with me."

Jen nodded, then stood and pulled D.J. into her arms. "I'm going to get dressed," she said. "You should take this time to get used to the fact we're coming with you. And not to your aunt and uncle's home."

With that, she turned and strutted back down the hall, determined to be useful in finding Madison and not left behind with members of his extended family, whom she'd never met.

KNOX FINISHED CLEANING up breakfast, still smiling at Jen's assertiveness, while she went to change.

His phone dinged repeatedly on the countertop beside the sink, alerting him to the mass of incoming texts from his auntie and cousins.

He'd missed family dinner last night and forgotten to call. Definite cause for alarm in the Winchester family, and apparently punishable by endless texts and voice messages. Friday night dinners were an unspoken necessity to anyone not on duty, and when he'd played hooky in the past, he'd always called to let his auntie down gently. He'd dropped the ball this time, and had some explaining to do as a result. Especially since everyone knew he was on vacation.

He opened a group text to save time, then sent a series of short messages relaying the gist of his situation. There was a moment of silence, presumably while they processed his answer. Then the dings began anew.

Announcing he'd stayed at Jen's house for her protection had incited a fresh round of questions about Jen from his aunt Rosa and his cousins' new wives. His brother and cousins, a private investigator and several lawmen, offered their assistance if he needed it.

He considered suggesting the men in his family take away their wives' phones, then recalled Jen announcing she was coming with him, after he'd told her she couldn't, and decided to concentrate on the problem at hand.

When Jen reappeared in a fitted T-shirt and stretchy pants that emphasized all his favorite aspects of a woman's body, he had to remind himself not to stare. And she wanted to lose weight? Was she nuts?

She slipped a baby sling around her torso and positioned D.J. inside. "We should ask the building manager about my new locks on our way out," she said.

Then she opened the door and was gone.

Knox rubbed his forehead with one heavy palm, while his phone continued dinging.

Jen would fit right in with the little female army

his family had recently accumulated, if he ever introduced her. And the women would surely try to recruit her if he did.

Chapter Six

Knox unlocked the doors to his truck and watched as Jen transferred D.J.'s car seat from her sedan to the back of his extended cab. The baby bounced contentedly in his sling against her chest. According to her building manager, the locksmith was on his way, and there would be a new set of keys in Jen's mailbox when she returned.

"I think we should have a cover story while we look for clues about Madison's disappearance," she said, fastening the complicated harness over her son. "We don't want to scare anyone who might know what happened to her by announcing you're the law. I don't know any criminals, but I'm positive they won't talk to you if you lead with that."

Knox smirked. She was explaining things to him as if this was what she did and he was along for the ride. "Is that right?"

"Yes. So, we should try to look like two friends who are out enjoying a day together," she said, closing the rear door and climbing onto the passenger seat. "When we question people, we'll tell them I'm her roommate and worried because she didn't come home."

He shot her a flat look across the cab. "I'm not a deputy sheriff today."

"Exactly."

"Wrong," he said. "I'm the law every day."

She turned her head to face him, unimpressed. "You're on vacation."

And what a vacation it is so far, he thought dryly. Then reversed out of the parking space without retort.

"Do you still have the power to arrest someone while on vacation?" she asked.

Knox rubbed his forehead, then stole a glance at her baby in his rearview mirror. That child wasn't going to get away with anything. His mother was too fond of calling the shots.

"Well?" she asked, forcing Knox to give what seemed like an obvious answer.

"Yes, I can still make arrests on vacation."

"There," she said. "We're all set."

He eased onto the road, unsure whether to laugh or sigh.

They rode in silence for several minutes, slowing as traffic increased near downtown.

Jen twisted at her waist, dramatically examining the scene around them. "What are you doing? The park is on the other end of town."

He rounded the next corner, then slid his truck into an empty spot outside a coffee shop. "True, but I usually take sandwiches with me to the park. Today, I'll have to pick them up from the deli. If we're making that pit stop before the park, we might as well take a look at the café Madison visited every morning while we're here."

Jen craned her neck for a look at the place on her right. "Coffee Cat?" She stared through each window, apparently trying to orient herself. "How do you know she came here?"

"Yep." He climbed out and rounded the tailgate.

Jen appeared on the sidewalk when he reached her door. She secured D.J. into her baby sling, then turned a determined look on Knox. "How do you know she came here every morning?" she asked again.

"Receipts in her bedroom trash." Knox held the door for Jen to enter the coffee shop. A blast of deliciously scented air washed over him as he crossed the threshold. "They were in the report Deputy Wence wrote up last night."

Jen furrowed her brow, then marched on, crossing large black-and-white-tiled flooring. She stopped at a counter near the back wall. The remainder of the small space was peppered by a dozen wooden table sets.

"Welcome to Coffee Cat," the guy behind the counter greeted. He was tall and lean, probably in his early twenties, with small blue eyes and an unfortunate nose. Knox hoped it was naturally crooked and not the result of one too many landed punches. His name tag said Ted. "What can I get you?"

Jen paused to look at the menu, then smiled warmly at Ted. "I'm not sure I can decide," she told him, tipping her head slightly to one side. "What would you recommend?"

Knox grimaced. Was she…flirting? With Ted? He gave the unremarkable barista another look and felt his frown deepen.

Ted smiled and made several complicated suggestions with words like *vanilla*, *macchiato* and *soy* in the titles. Jen moved along the counter with him once she'd made a decision, watching as he worked.

"My friend recommended this place," she said. "She comes here all the time. Says it's the best. Maybe you know her. Do you work a lot of mornings?"

"Five days a week," he said proudly, beaming as he foamed up her drink. "I don't usually have time to talk though. It can be really busy on weekdays."

Jen nodded, thoughtfully. "My friend's name is Madison. She's tall and thin, really pretty, with long black hair I'd kill for. She probably wears scrubs when she comes in. She works at a clinic downtown."

Ted passed her the coffee, then rang up the order. "The place on Market Street?"

"That's the one. Do you remember a woman like the one I described coming in here a lot?" Jen pressed, digging for her wallet. She stretched and shifted, reaching around the baby attached to her middle.

"Not really," Ted said. "Why?"

Knox groaned inwardly, then met them at the register, unable to watch any longer. "Hey, can I get a plain black coffee?" he asked. "Put hers on my bill." He looked at Jen, his wallet already in hand. "I've got this." He passed Ted some cash, then fixed his most authoritative stare on the man with kitty whiskers embroidered across his apron. "We need to know about the woman, so think hard. She's missing."

Ted blinked. "What?"

"Missing," Knox repeated, turning his cell phone to face the younger man. A photo of Madison centered the screen. Knox had pulled it from her social media the night before and saved it for this purpose.

Ted frowned, dragging his eyes from the image. "Who are you? How do I know you aren't looking for her with nefarious intent?"

Knox snorted. *Nefarious intent.* Who was this kid? "I'll give you twenty bucks to tell me what you know about her. Answer now, or I'll offer the cash to someone else who works here instead."

Jen gasped, and he slid her a sideways look in warning.

She'd been right to suggest he not announce himself as a lawman to everyone they met. People got tight-lipped when they knew a deputy sheriff was involved, and this kid looked exactly like one of those people.

Not surprisingly, Ted took the money. "I know her," he said. "She always ordered herbal tea or a bottle of water. Sometimes a fruit-and-yogurt par-

fait or a bagel. She sat at the same table every time."
He pointed to an empty two-seater near the window.

Knox nodded. "Was she always alone?"

Ted passed him a plain coffee. "Yeah, but I haven't
seen her for a couple days. Is she really missing?"

"Yes," Jen said, her voice going painfully soft.
"Thank you for the information."

Ted opened the register to make change, but Knox
waved him off, then led the way to the table in question. It felt good to be back in charge.

Jen watched him as they sat. "What now? We already knew she came here."

He cast his gaze through the tinted glass. "She always sat at the window. We didn't know that, and the
next logical question is, why? To people watch? Anyone specific? If so, who was she watching and why?"

Jen pulled D.J. from the sling and arranged him
on her lap, so he could take in the views. "You're
frowning again," she said. "What are you thinking?"

Knox worked his jaw, trying and failing to change
his expression. "Madison ordered caffeine-free tea
and bottled water on a daily basis. That doesn't
strike me as befitting the profile of someone seeking comfort outside themselves. Those are healthy,
non-indulgent choices."

"Not exactly hallmarks of an illegal drug user,
you mean?"

"No, and something else is bugging me," he said.
"Madison worked full-time. How many days a week

was that? A standard Monday through Friday, or weekends too?"

Jen puzzled a moment, turning her mug slowly on the table. "Monday through Friday. Why?"

"The receipts in her trash say she was here every day this week and last. This place isn't in your neighborhood, and the coffee isn't that good," he said, making a face at the brew he'd barely sipped. "So, why go all the way downtown if she didn't have to?"

"To sit alone in front of this window," Jen said, turning her attention back to the glass. She lifted the mug and shifted on her seat, struggling to enjoy her foamy drink without lifting it directly over her baby.

Knox smiled. "Mind if I hold him so you can finish that eight-dollar monstrosity?"

She cocked a curious brow, before relief swept over her face. "Sure." She handed her baby carefully to Knox. "I would've paid for my own drink," she said. "I didn't mean to stick you with the bill, and for the record, I don't normally get something with so many bells and whistles. I was trying to get the barista to like me so he'd answer my questions."

Knox snorted a quiet laugh, curling D.J. against his chest. "You raised that poor kid's self-esteem to new heights."

She laughed, then sipped her drink with a sigh. "He didn't tell me anything until you butted in and intimidated him. Thank you for that, by the way, and for the coffee."

"Don't mention it." Knox made a few faces at D.J.,

and the kid gave a wide toothless grin. Knox chuckled. Kids were funny, and his family was adding new ones to the roster left and right.

The little man in his arms looked a lot like Jen. The set of his lips and shape of his eyes were all hers, but the rest... The color of his tawny skin, dark hair and brown eyes were all Dylan. Knox could see his friend in the angle of D.J.'s jaw and the mischief in his stare. If he was anything like his father in personality, Jen would have her work cut out for her during the teenage years. Though he was sure she'd manage just fine.

"You're good with him," she said, crossing her legs beneath the table and bumping her foot against his. "Planning on having one of your own someday? Or are you too single to think about that just yet?"

He grinned. "I'd like to have a few, eventually. My brother, Cruz, and I were raised to be friends, not just brothers, and when we lost our mama back in high school, it was the bond she'd created that got us through it. I'd like to pass that gift on to kids of my own. I think family is everything. It's pretty great to know someone always has your back."

Something tilted in Jen's expression, sending a tug of sadness through Knox's heart. He'd nearly forgotten her folks were in Florida and her dad was ill.

"How's your dad?" he asked. "You mentioned he isn't well."

She shrugged. "He had a heart attack a few years back. Hasn't been the same since, but he's still with us, so I'm thankful for that. I'm sorry about your mama," she added. "I didn't know."

Knox's throat tightened the way it always did when someone voiced those words. "Thanks."

An older woman in business-casual attire appeared from the back of the café and made her way around the tables, greeting patrons and making chit-chat. Her lack of apron gave the impression of authority. Her genuine interest and obvious familiarity with the guests made Knox suspect she was the owner. The shop's logo was emblazoned on her chest, but she wasn't wearing a name tag.

"Is that the manager?" Jen asked, noticing the same woman who'd caught Knox's eye.

He smiled and lifted a hand when she headed to their table. "One way to find out," he whispered.

"Good morning," she said brightly upon approach. "What a lovely family. And who is this?" she asked the baby in his arms.

"This is D.J.," Knox answered, "and Jen." He tipped his head to the blushing woman seated across from him. "I'm Knox. It's nice to meet you," he said, not bothering to correct her misinterpretation of their group status. "This is our first time here. It's nice."

"Thank you," she said. "I'm Cat."

Knox frowned. "Coffee Cat."

"That's me." She pointed to the logo on her shirt.

Jen laughed, and the bubbly sound warmed him. "Do you come in every morning?" she asked.

"Almost," Cat said.

Knox flipped his phone over on the table, quickly selecting Madison's picture once more. "This is our friend," he said, lifting the device in Cat's direction. "She's missing. We know she came here a lot and sat at this table, but we're hoping you can tell us more."

"We're retracing her steps," Jen added. "She's my best friend, and she vanished last night."

Cat's expression fell. "I know Madison. Have you called the police?"

Knox nodded. "They're looking for her too."

The older woman covered her mouth with one hand. "Wow. Okay. Let me think. I've spoken to her many times, but never about anything substantial. She always had a notebook and pencil. She sat at this table and doodled." She bit her bottom lip, eyes roaming as she thought. "She took pictures sometimes."

Jen wrinkled her nose. "Selfies?"

"No, through the window. People watching, I guess." Cat motioned to the road outside. "I assumed she did that so she could finish the drawings after she left."

Knox stared at the parking lot and buildings across the street. The clinic where Madison worked was on the next block, and probably accessible from a visible alley. He rocked onto his hip, adjusting D.J. in his arms as he freed his wallet. He flipped the leather bifold open and produced a business card for Cat. "If you think of anything else, or if anyone comes in here asking about Madison. Or us," he added belatedly, as the thought occurred. They were seated before a giant window, after all. "Give me a call."

Cat's lips parted as she read the card. She nodded, eyes filled with concern as she tucked the little rectangle into the pocket of her khaki pants and moved on to the next table.

Jen released a deep breath. "How much do you want to bet Madison was watching the alleyway, and that it leads to the clinic?"

"Yep." Knox put his wallet away, prepared to ask Jen if she was ready to go, but she was already on her feet, waiting for him.

Chapter Seven

Jen followed Knox across the street, exhausted by the weight of the day. It was still early, but they'd already accomplished so much. Normally, she'd still be in her pajamas, playing on the floor with D.J. Today, however, she'd confirmed the locksmith, traveled downtown, learned new things about Madison's days prior to her disappearance and she was now on her way to talk to Madison's coworkers. Was this what Knox's life was like every day?

She peeked at the handsome protector beside her, wondering how he usually spent his time. She had so many questions about his life. None of the answers were any of her business, but she appreciated how easily he answered everything she was brave enough to ask. Knox Winchester was inarguably gorgeous, but he was a lot more than a pretty face. He was protective, compassionate and kind. Plus, he wasn't afraid to cook or clean. Definite bonus points for those. Unlike so many men she'd known, Knox was capable, and he didn't wait for someone else to do something he could do himself.

She tried not to think about how much she liked all the new things she'd learned about him. Or how refreshing it was to hear him talk about his family. He obviously loved his aunt, uncle, brother and cousins. And he wanted children of his own one day. Her heart fluttered nonsensically at the thought, and her gaze drifted back to her son in his arms.

Knox held D.J. so confidently. He looked natural with a baby against his chest. Maybe there were a lot of kids in his family. She tucked that question away for later, along with all the other things she wanted to know about him, but wasn't sure how or when it was appropriate to ask.

Madison's disappearance loomed heavily in Jen's heart and mind. Each time she thought too long or hard about her budding attachment to Knox, the reminder of why their paths had crossed again hit like a sledge. And she felt like the worst kind of friend.

He turned to her as shame and guilt coiled in her gut, causing her steps to stutter. For a moment, she wondered if he could read her mind. "Ready?" he asked, pausing on the corner.

She nodded, and Knox offered his hand.

"Coffee Cat assumed we were a family," he said. "Maybe that's our cover story. Seems like a good one to me."

Jen gaped at his hand. Her heart kicked into overdrive at the rush of unbidden images from her dream.

Those big hands in her hair, cupping her cheeks and drawing her close.

She was an absolutely terrible friend. How could she be thinking of this when Madison was missing?

Knox's smile fell. "You suggested we come up with a cover this morning." Knox lowered his hand, concern wrinkling his brow. "Sorry. I didn't mean to suggest…" His words trailed off, and his sharp green eyes turned to D.J. in his arms. "I wasn't trying to… No one will ever take Dylan's place," he said finally.

"I know," she said, slipping her hand into his. "My thoughts are all over the place, but I wasn't thinking anything like that." Her cheeks heated as their palms aligned, and the roughness of his calloused skin scraped deliciously against hers. She hadn't held a man's hand in more than a year, and the act felt so incredibly personal, so intimate, it sent little lightning bolts down her spine. *Get a hold of yourself*, she scolded internally, closing her eyes briefly against the intensity.

"You okay?" he asked, the low tenor and attentive tone of his voice nearly buckling her knees.

She wasn't even close to okay. The weight of the last year, of Dylan's sudden death before that and the complete emotional fatigue of being a single mother felt like a thousand-pound weight on her shoulders. Madison's disappearance might be the thing that pushed Jen's precarious state over the edge.

Except she couldn't let that happen. Not for her sake, but for her son's.

"Jen?" Knox pressed, his cool green eyes appraising her in the sunlight.

"I'm fine," she said. Certain he could see straight through her thinly veiled bravado, she added, "Nervous."

He tugged her more closely to his side, then winked down at her.

D.J. smiled and cooed.

"You've got this," Knox promised. "And I've got you."

Warmth spread through her at his simple, comforting words. She squeezed his fingers in thanks, drawing on his cool confidence and reminding herself she wasn't alone.

Knox smiled and made small talk as they moved swiftly toward their destination. Though she didn't think the smile quite reached his eyes. Instead, he seemed to be taking in the details around them, likely registering dozens of things that would never reveal themselves to her.

She did her best to seem as unhurried and casual as he did, especially when they passed others on the sidewalk, or coming and going from storefronts and shops.

When they reached the clinic, he released her hand, then opened and held the door for her.

Their bodies brushed in the narrow space as she passed. The heady scent of him, coupled with his nearness, fogged up her brain as she stepped inside.

The clinic was small but busy. Its pale blue walls

were lined in commercial seating, and every chair
was occupied. A sign on the door had identified the
general practitioners as Michael Martz and Robert
Abel.

Jen led the way to a welcome desk on the far wall,
positioned beside a closed door leading to offices
and exam rooms. A blonde woman in maroon scrubs
greeted her with a smile. According to the rectangular badge on her chest, her name was Katie.

Katie set a clipboard on the counter between them
and tapped one finger to the empty line at the bottom. With her free hand, she motioned to her head-
set, indicating she was on a call.

If Jen had been there as a patient, she would've
written her name, time of arrival and appointment
on the line. Instead, she shook her head slightly and
smiled back.

Eventually, the receptionist finished her call and
offered an apologetic grin. "Sorry to keep you waiting. It's been a busy morning." Her gaze traveled
from Jen to Knox and D.J. The look turned blatantly
appreciative as she took in the tall drink of water on
Jen's right. "Who are we seeing today?"

Jen refused to roll her eyes, so she closed them
in a long blink before refocusing. She was willing
to bet he got those looks everywhere he went, and
given the cluelessness on his face at the moment, he
probably didn't even know he was being ogled. "We
don't have an appointment," Jen said. "We're hoping

to ask you a couple questions. My roommate, Madison, works here."

Katie's expression turned quizzical, then thrilled as she pulled her gaze back to Jen. "So you're Jen!" She beamed. "It's so nice to meet you. I'm Katie. This must be D.J."

Jen cast a proud look at her son, content and drowsy in Knox's arms. "The one and only." Her heart simultaneously swelled and broke with the knowledge Madison had spoken frequently enough about them that Katie would recall their names.

"I hear so much about you both," Katie said. "I feel as if I know you already. How can I help?"

"We're actually looking for Madison," Jen said, her throat tightening on the words.

Katie gave a sad smile. "She's not on the schedule today. She almost never works weekends. You didn't know?"

"I do," Jen said. "But she's not home, and I don't know where she is. I'd hoped you could shed some light. She never came home last night."

The other woman blanched. "Madison is missing?" Her eyes widened, and her mouth formed a tight line. She turned her face away, looking at something beyond Jen's sight, hidden by the wall that separated them.

"When was the last time you saw her?" Jen asked, pulling the other woman's attention back to her.

"Earlier this week." Katie wet her lips, then leaned forward slightly, tipping over the counter. "She didn't come in for her scheduled shift yesterday. I left her a voice mail, but she didn't return it. I thought she'd just overslept or forgotten."

Jen's heart pounded as the news registered. She'd thought Madison had only been missing since the previous evening. Was it possible she'd been missing all day?

Knox moved in closer, angling himself against the counter and sweeping his gaze over the waiting room behind them. "How did she seem to you the last time you saw her?" he asked.

Katie chewed her lip, looking away from them once more. He tracked something Jen couldn't see. "I don't know," Katie said. "She was fine. Quiet and busy. She handled the files and paperwork, so we didn't get to talk much." She turned forward and straightened, no longer their coconspirator. "I'm sure she'll turn up. Probably just needed a day off."

Knox rested a hand on the small of Jen's back, silently comforting her once more. "Maybe," he told Katie. "Any chance we can speak with one of the doctors? Maybe they have some insight. Or perhaps another one of your coworkers. We're open to any information that can help us find her. We don't want to leave any stone unturned."

Jen looked up at him, sensing the subtle authority he'd added to his words.

Katie looked away again, eyes darting and expression turning troubled. "Not today. Drs. Martz and Abel are swamped, and to be honest, Madison was incredibly private. She barely talked to anyone."

"But she told you about me and D.J.," Jen said. "You might know more than you realize. Did she say anything recently that struck you as odd or out of character? Did she seem more distracted or less talkative?"

Katie shook her head while Jen spoke. "No. I'm sorry. I can't help you. You can make an appointment with Dr. Martz or Dr. Abel if you'd like, but I really need to get back to work." Her tone was congenial, but forced, and the ease with which she'd greeted them had thoroughly dissolved.

Knox removed his wallet again, jostling D.J. while he freed a business card and passed it to Katie. "If you think of anything, let me know."

A little gasp escaped her lips as she read the card, then moved it quickly to her pocket.

Knox used his massive palm on Jen's back to guide her away.

She didn't speak until they were on the sidewalk. "That was it?" she asked, shocked and astounded. "Why didn't you ask her more questions? And if you were going to let her know you were a deputy, why didn't you insist she talk? Or at least demand an interview with the rest of the staff? She was clearly hiding something. Even I could see that, and I don't have any of the training you've had."

Knox nudged her forward, not answering her questions. He steered her to the end of the block, then across the street when the signal changed. "I'm on vacation," he said, motioning her to a bench at the edge of a tree-lined park one hundred yards or so from the clinic. "The sheriff's department will do all the official legwork. I'm just nudging a few fence posts to see if a gate opens."

Jen sat, though she wanted to pace, or return to the clinic and ask more questions. "I don't know what that means," she said, reaching for D.J. as Knox lowered his tall frame onto the seat at her side.

"It means I'm just nosing around, putting out feelers and testing the waters. If anything seems amiss, I'll report it to the deputies on this case. If not, we'll keep looking." He relaxed one long arm across the wooden slat behind her shoulders, assuming a casual position, when all she wanted to do was scream in frustration.

"That receptionist knew something," she said. "Did you see how nervous she got? And what was she looking at on the other side of the wall?"

"Agreed," Knox said, "and I'm not sure."

"Did you see her face when she read your card?"

He nodded, eyes fixed on something in the distance.

Jen tracked his gaze to the small parking lot outside the clinic. The lot butted up to an alley, barely visible from her position. There were eight cars divided neatly in two rows. Two high-end sedans, and six cars people could generally afford.

Before Jen could ask Knox what he was looking at, specifically, a figure appeared in the lot.

"Looks like something shook loose," Knox said.

Jen watched in awe as Katie darted to a small red hatchback, dropped behind the wheel, then zoomed away.

Chapter Eight

Jen watched as Knox navigated to the clinic's website on his phone, then searched for a listing of the staff. It only took a moment to find the group photo on the practice's About page, alongside a description of how the doctors met and why they chose to be one of the first new businesses in the revitalized downtown. According to the site, they wanted to be *conveniently located for the people of their community, with better accessibility and extended office hours*. They further claimed to pride themselves on hiring locals and seeking graduates of area schools.

"Madison's not in the photo," Jen said. "She hasn't worked there long, that's probably why, but I think that's Katie." She pointed to a slightly heavier woman than the one they'd met, with longer, blonder hair, but it was definitely the receptionist.

Knox swiped the page away and switched to his texting app. He curved forward over the device, creating shade on the screen, then began to tap a message.

"What are you doing?" Jen asked.

"Reaching out to the sheriff's department."

She'd assumed as much, but had hoped for a more thorough explanation. She chewed her lip as she processed what she'd just seen. "Why do you think Katie ran off like that? The waiting room was packed. She even mentioned how busy they were. Do you think we scared her?" Jen rewound the conversation, weighing all the things that might've triggered Katie's change in demeanor and led to her leaving work so quickly. A new and hopeful thought burst into mind. She inhaled deeply at the possibility. "What if she knows where Madison is? We should follow her." Jen looked in the direction the little red hatchback had gone, but it was lost to a sea of taillights. Her newly gained hope plummeted. There was no chance of catching her now. Knox's truck was still parked outside Coffee Cat, a full block away.

Knox stood and offered her his hand. "I requested an address on Katie. We should have it by the time we get to my truck."

"We're going to her house?" Jen asked, adrenaline rising, then colliding with a discouraging possibility. "What if she didn't go home?" What if she knew where Madison was and was on her way there? And Jen had missed her chance to follow.

"There's only one way to find out," Knox said, wiggling his still-waiting fingers.

She accepted his hand, and they headed back to his pickup at double the pace they'd left it.

Twenty minutes later, they arrived outside an older

home in a working-class neighborhood. The hatchback was in the driveway.

Knox led the way to the door, and Jen tried to keep her cool as the hope of seeing Madison again welled in her.

She kissed D.J.'s hair, inhaled the scent of him and played with his chubby, dimpled fingers, working to keep her heart rate calm, despite the number of questions stampeding through her mind. And she prayed she wasn't carrying her baby into a dangerous situation.

Knox rang the bell, and the curtain moved in the window beside the door. When no one answered, he knocked.

Jen counted silently, both to calm her nerves and to gauge the passing time. Thankfully, Knox didn't make a move to leave, because Jen would've stubbornly stood there all night if it meant gaining information about Madison's disappearance. The passing seconds felt like hours as they waited. The frightening truth was that Katie could easily deny them another conversation. And there wasn't anything Jen could do about that.

Four seconds later, the sound of a sliding chain lock was followed by the turn of a deadbolt. The front door sucked open before them, and Katie appeared. She released a heavy breath, then stepped away, offering them entrance.

She closed the door quickly once they were inside, then reengaged the locks. "What are you doing here?" she asked, looking through the front window before turning a deep frown on them.

Knox offered a kind smile, his keen eyes seeming to take inventory of their surroundings. "We saw you leave the clinic in a hurry, and wondered if you were okay," he said.

Jen bit the insides of her cheeks, thankful he'd taken the lead. She wasn't sure what to say. They'd already frightened Katie once, and Knox was probably used to interrogating suspects.

Jen gave the home a careful scan, following Knox's example and hoping to see something to indicate Madison was nearby.

Katie crossed her arms and shook her head. "You're stalking me now? That's illegal. You should know." She fixed Knox with an angry stare.

He lifted his palms in response. "I'm not here as a lawman. We're here as friends because we think Madison is in trouble."

"We were at the park when you left work," Jen offered. She kissed her baby's head, hoping to convey the idea that maybe they'd been there innocently, getting a little fresh air for her son. "We saw you racing away and worried that we'd upset you. Or that maybe you're in trouble too."

Katie's gaze jumped erratically from Jen to Knox. She wrapped her arms around her middle and stepped back, unsure. "I had a headache, and I came home to rest."

Knox nodded. "The clinic was really busy. That must've been a terrible headache."

"It was," she said.

Jen took a few steps, rocking gently to soothe her baby. She gave the room another long look, desperate for something to stand out. The furnishings were sparse. The space was in need of some general repairs, but everything was clean and cared for. It was the home of a working woman just getting by. Jen's gaze landed on a set of photos across Katie's mantel. All were images of her and a small boy. "You have a son?" she asked. From the photos, Jen would guess the child was probably eight or nine.

Katie nodded, tightening her hold on herself. "His father has custody, but he stays here on the weekends and during extended school breaks. I was in some trouble when I had him, and it was the right decision at the time."

Jen's heart ached at the thought of only seeing D.J. on weekends. She hated the humility and shame in Katie's voice as she explained the situation. Everyone made mistakes, and the woman before them was clearly working to right hers, whatever they'd been.

"I've got a good life now," Katie said. "And a good job. I can't afford any trouble."

Knox's eyes narrowed. "What sort of trouble do you think we're going to connect you to?"

Her skin paled, and her mouth opened. She looked to Jen again, maybe for help, but as much as Jen could empathize with another young mother, Madison was missing, and she needed to be found.

"I don't know w-what you're talking about," Katie said.

"Look," Jen interrupted, voice pleading as she moved forward, trading a sideways glance with Knox. "We don't know what's going on, but something is obviously wrong. I thought I was Madison's only local friend, but clearly she talks to you too. And it seems like you know something about where she is, or what's happening with her. If you do, then we need to know that too. I love her, and I'm scared. I don't want to lose her."

Katie took another step back. "Madison and I weren't friends. We didn't talk, and I don't know anything."

"Anything about what?" Jen asked, the words dragging out in desperation. "What is happening? And why won't you tell me? Madison could be hurt or scared. Or worse," she added, her throat going dry at the memory of how quickly a human life could end. "Did you know Madison lost her husband last year?" she asked. "She's been through so much already, and I just want to find her and bring her home."

Katie shook her head slowly, eyes glistening with unshed tears. "I'm sorry." Her gaze flickered to the photos of her son on the mantel. "I can't help you."

"We found drugs in the apartment," Jen blurted.

Knox stiffened at her side and reached for her wrist, giving it a warning squeeze.

Katie's eyes widened.

"If she had a problem," Jen said, pivoting her interrogation, "I can get her help. She doesn't have to go through it alone."

"What kind of drugs?" Katie asked, her arms falling limply to her sides.

"MX-10," Knox answered, taking over at the mention of the drug. "It's become an epidemic in this area, and with Madison's history of depression, we understand she's a prime candidate for use. Like I said before, we're here as friends, and we're worried."

Katie blinked slowly, her eyes suddenly distant and unfocused. "I can't help you," she said, her voice flat and defeated. For the first time since their arrival, she looked truly ill. "I'm sorry, but you have to go. I need to lie down."

Knox towed Jen back to the front door by her wrist. "I hope you feel better soon," he said. "We're sorry to have bothered you."

Jen cast a final pleading look at the other woman, hoping Katie would say something more, anything more.

But she only closed the door behind them.

KNOX WALKED JEN and D.J. back to his truck and helped them inside. Then he powered the windows down and started the engine. There were fewer than a dozen cars visible on the street. Driveways were empty, as they often were at this hour in neighborhoods like these. The homes were old and in need of repair, but the lawns, porches and sidewalks were neat as a pin. These were the places where people worked for what they had, and they took care of the things in their charge. Most of the vehicles in sight seemed appropriate for the area. The newest of older-model cars was parked nearly a block away, dark and motionless, with a paper thirty-day tag in the rear window.

Katie and her home fit the area's profile. If he had to guess by the scars on her arms, she'd been a drug user at one time, and that was likely the reason she didn't have custody of her son. Knox could only hope she wasn't using anymore.

When they were safely inside, Knox buckled up and started the engine, then drove around the block and cut back to where they'd started, using an alley between homes across the street from Katie's place. He shifted into Park, this time with an excellent view of the entire block.

Jen didn't ask any questions when he'd driven away, or when he settled the engine once more. Instead, she mixed a small bottle and passed it to her baby. Then offered Knox a granola bar.

He smiled. "You keep snacks in your purse? My grandmama used to do that. Are there tissues in your bra too?"

"Wouldn't you like to know," she answered, pulling a pack of peanuts from her bag next.

It was unsettling how much he'd like to know what

was in her bra, but he kept that to himself. Instead, he marveled at her preparedness.

She caught him staring and frowned. "You're still thinking about what's in my bra. Aren't you?"

"I was thinking you're like a cross between Mary Poppins and a Scout. With your bag of necessities, always ready to troubleshoot." He grinned. It was fun to see Jen in action, unafraid and wholly determined. Despite the difficult circumstances, she was headstrong and steadfast. He was sure plenty of people would've cracked, quit or had a breakdown under the pressure, but not her.

Unexpected admiration tugged at him.

She tore the peanut package open and shook a few nuts into her hand. "I'm a single mom. The superhero of our day. It's a heavy cape, but someone has to wear it." She lifted her chin and smiled. "And planning ahead is a top-notch life hack. You should try it."

"I plan ahead," he said. "I keep a go bag in the truck, or I'd be wearing yesterday's clothes right now."

She flicked her blue gaze to him. "Where are your snacks?"

He laughed, then opened his granola bar. It was nice that she thought of everything, but part of him hated that she had to. She shouldn't have to be so wholly self-reliant. Everyone needed someone. Didn't they? The idea of being that person for her popped into his mind, and it felt nicer than it should.

Katie's front door opened, pulling his thoughts back to the moment.

"She's leaving," Jen said, pointing through the windshield, in case Knox had somehow missed it.

Katie hurried down the porch steps and to her car, struggling to manage several overnight bags.

"Looks like her head feels better," he said.

"Looks like she's going somewhere," Jen said. "Is she leaving town? That definitely means we were right. She knows something."

"Probably," he said, already tapping the update into a text for dispatch. Preferably a uniform who was on duty, unlike himself, and not hauling a civilian and a baby around. "I'm letting another deputy know."

"What?" Jen gasped. "We're already here. We have to follow her. What if she's on her way to Madison? What if she knows where she is?"

"Another deputy will—"

"Follow her," Jen said, gripping his arm. "Let another deputy take over when they catch up, but don't lose her."

Unable to argue the reasonable suggestion, Knox shifted into Drive and eased onto the road behind Katie's fast-disappearing car.

Chapter Nine

Knox hurried along the residential streets, monitoring the rearview mirror, sidewalks and scene around him, while keeping an eye on the little hatchback. He mentally tallied the traffic violations as he kept his distance, trying not to alert her to the tail. So far, she was blatantly speeding, had rolled through two stop signs at intersections and had come unnervingly close to leaving her lane a number of times. If she was using her phone while driving, she needed to pull over before she caused an accident, but he was too far back to know for sure.

He radioed their new location each time she changed direction, maintaining communication with the deputy assigned to intervene. Jen would be unhappy if backup didn't arrive soon, because Knox drew the line at putting her and D.J. in danger to follow Katie any farther than absolutely necessary. And he had no plans to run a red light or make any sort of illegal turns in the name of following Katie.

"Something scared her," Jen said, breaking his

reverie. Her voice was calm, apparently unfazed by Katie's erratic driving.

"Yeah," he said. "Us." Knox slowed as they reached the main roads through town, putting two more cars between them. "We confronted her at work, then followed her home and insinuated we knew she had information on a missing woman who was in possession of MX-10." It was too late now, but he wished Jen had left the drug detail out of Katie's questioning.

Jen pursed her lips. "She could've just talked. You gave her your card. She knows you're a deputy and you could've helped her."

"People who've had trouble with the law in the past are extremely slow to warm up to the possibility we won't arrest them again," he said. "Even if they aren't doing anything wrong. And she's got a lot on the line with her son's custody situation."

Jen seemed to consider that. "We don't know her previous trouble was with the law."

Not yet, Knox thought, *but we soon will*. Katie was receiving a thorough background check while they kept tabs on her in traffic.

Jen twisted to peek into the back seat. "Out like a light," she said, facing forward with a smile. "The old bottle-and-a-car-ride combination never fails."

Knox couldn't stop his smile, despite his agitation with Katie's driving. "You're an old pro at motherhood already. That must feel good."

"It doesn't feel bad," she said, as she gripped the dashboard on their next turn.

Katie took her next left turn in front of oncoming traffic. Horns honked and drivers hollered.

Knox moved carefully into the turn lane, positioning himself to follow her, when it was safe.

"I want to go through Madison's things when we get home," Jen said, completely at ease beside him. "I thought about it last night, but I didn't want to invade her privacy more than the deputies already had. I don't care about any of that right now. I think she's in serious trouble, and if we find her and bring her home safely, she won't complain about how we get it done. She'll just be glad to be home."

"Agreed," Knox said, thankful she'd chosen an activity that would keep her and D.J. someplace confined and safe. "You know her best, so there's a chance you'll notice something Wence and Van didn't."

"I'm curious about the notebook and pencil Coffee Cat mentioned," she said. "I've never known Madison to draw or doodle. I think it's more likely she was making notes. She's detailed to a fault."

"Another good idea," Knox said, silently cursing the deputy who hadn't caught up with them yet. "I'd like to compare Madison's work schedule with the receipts from the coffee shop. See if there's a pattern in the dates that stands out."

Ahead of them, the little red hatchback accelerated through another intersection as the light turned red. The more cautious drivers in front of Knox stopped, as did he.

A cruiser appeared in oncoming traffic, and Knox radioed the information on Katie's turn.

The cruiser's lights went on.

"Better late than never," Knox muttered.

"Only if he catches her," Jen said.

Knox hit his turn signal as the cruiser headed in the direction Katie had gone. When the light was green for him again, Knox rerouted the truck toward Jen's apartment.

"Wait. Don't go home yet," Jen said, a note of alarm in her tone. "We still have to visit the park."

Knox nearly hung his head. He'd forgotten about that, and he preferred the idea of getting Jen and D.J. back into their building. "We never stopped at the deli," he said, offering a flimsy excuse to skip the outing. "I usually bring sandwiches."

"Good thing everyone likes Burger Haven," she said, pulling a set of gift cards from her magic bag.

THEY CRUISED INTO the park's parking lot several minutes later, armed with five of everything on the fast-food restaurant's dollar menu.

Jen slipped a sleeping D.J. into her sling, then shut the truck door softly, careful not to wake him. She inhaled the warm summer air and sent up another prayer for Madison's sake. Her heart ached at the thought of how this search might end, and she feared for Katie too. Something was wrong, and it seemed as if Madison and Katie were in on it.

Why hadn't Madison let Jen in on it?

A soft snore rose from the baby at her chest, and Jen knew the answer to her question. Madison would never do anything to endanger D.J., so she must've known what she was doing was wrong. Yet, Madison wasn't the kind of woman who did things she knew were wrong. It simply wasn't who she was. Which only made the last two days seem more impossibly surreal. It was as if Jen and D.J. had left the community center after swim class and walked into a completely different world.

Knox strode confidently ahead of her, two handled shopping bags full of food in his massive grip.

Jen hung back, not wanting to make the group Knox planned to speak with uncomfortable. It seemed to her that most people were guarded when being asked uncomfortable questions. Like, if they'd witnessed a gunman in the park last night, for example. A park where many of them might live. A thread of fear weaved through her at the thought. If any of them had seen something awful happen, and was brave enough to talk about it, would they be in danger for snitching? If the shooter somehow found out, where could the witnesses hide?

She offered a warm smile as she put some distance between Knox and her, and moved toward the carousel Madison loved.

She approached slowly, keeping watch on the people in her periphery and making sure not to leave Knox's line of sight. A series of metal blockade fences about four feet tall surrounded the antique ride. She crouched to look beneath the metal carousel floor. It was dark, and she used her cell phone's flashlight to aid her eyes, but only found rocks and dirt.

Next, she examined the horses, but there wasn't anything amiss there either.

Eventually, she reached the far side of the carousel, where four-by-eight-foot sections of plywood had been erected and signs announcing the restoration project and timeline were posted. She trailed her fingers along the makeshift wall, thinking it seemed like a good place to hide in the dark. Even with the security lights on, the barrier would've created long shadows, like the one around the tree where the gunman had appeared.

Jen shivered at the memory, her gaze falling briefly and catching on a thin silvery line. She crouched for a closer look and found pencil marks on the makeshift wall. The marks were hasty and scrawled, but she recognized them as words. As names. And Madison's name was underlined. Below that was a single word.

Abel.

That was also the name of one of the doctors from the clinic. Dr. Michael Martz and Dr. Robert Abel.

"Knox!" The word burst from her lips, causing D.J. to flinch. "Shh," she cooed in apology. She stroked his back comfortingly as she rushed in her protector's direction.

Knox's eyes were on hers, his body moving toward her before she'd taken more than a few steps of her own. "What's wrong?"

"Look." She led him back to the compressed wood, then crouched and pointed to the list. She accessed her phone's camera and took several photos for later.

Knox did the same, then texted his pictures to the sheriff's department. When he stood once more, he caught her with a compassionate look. "We need to tread lightly from here. This could be a crime scene."

Jen froze, her limbs stiff with panic as she nodded.

Knox walked the immediate area slowly, carefully, scrutinizing the area between the list and the gravel access road. He lowered into a squat several feet away.

Jen's heart hammered as he raised his phone once more, this time to his ear.

He announced himself, then added, "I need a deputy at Carousel Park. We've got drag marks, and signs of a struggle."

Jen drifted in his direction, pulled by the tethers of fear and heartbreak. Flashes of unspeakable scenarios blinked into her mind like a fun house strobe light. A faceless attacker. Madison's terror. Her useless fight.

Her abduction.

The world began to shimmer in Jen's periphery, and the air seemed suddenly too thin.

Knox cursed as he stepped carefully into a patch of tall grass along the road's edge. He pulled a set of blue gloves from his back pocket and snapped them on before retrieving something for inspection.

The ground tilted beneath her as the item came clearly into view.

Madison's cell phone.

Chapter Ten

Jen stared at the phone in Knox's gloved hand. Her gaze traveled to the drag marks in the soft earth, then to the list written on the plywood beside her. The names were invisible from only a few feet away, even in the sunlight. Madison had had her pencil with her, but there wasn't any sign of her notebook. Would they find that here somewhere too?

"Looks like it," Knox said, still speaking on the phone, and drawing her eyes back to him.

He stood at the base of a utility pole, head tipped back and eyes skyward. His free hand shielded the sun. "They might be owned by the construction company in charge of the renovations, but there's definitely a security camera, and it's pointed directly at the carousel."

She followed his gaze up the pole to the object in question.

"How soon can you get out here?" he asked. "All right. We'll wait."

Knox disconnected and tucked the phone into his

pocket. He turned to Jen with his hands on his hips. "You okay?"

"No." Her roommate was missing, apparently dragged away from a park at night. Probably by the man Jen had seen with a gun. Nothing about this was all right.

Knox headed for her, arms opening at the last moment, before wrapping her and D.J. in a hug. "I'm sorry you're going through this."

She leaned into him, resting her head on his chest and cradling her son between them. "I don't know how to feel or how to process," she said, emotion welling in her chest and throat. "I'm glad for the evidence, because I know it's what we need, but I'm horrified by what this means." She struggled to even her breaths and calm her racing heart. "Do drag marks mean she's…" She paused, the constricting lump in her throat making it impossible to finish the gruesome thought.

"No. Madison was most likely unconscious, but alive at the time," he said, answering her unfinished question. "Otherwise, there wouldn't have been a reason to take her."

Jen nodded, finding logic and hope in the awful explanation.

As long as Madison was alive, there was still time to save her.

"This is all good news," Knox said, his breath blowing against her hair. "The lab will send folks down here to make casts of the shoe prints for anal-

ysis. They'll come back with height and weight estimates of her abductor. Tech will work on getting her
phone unlocked. And with a little luck, the security
camera recorded the whole thing."

Jen pulled herself together and stepped away.
Everyone had a job to do. Including her. She just
needed her marching orders. "What now?"

"Now, we wait another few minutes for the crime
scene team to arrive. I have a few more questions for
the folks I was just talking to, then you and I will take
D.J. home and wait for more news. Sound good?"

"Okay."

Knox wrapped his arm across her shoulders, pulling her close as they moved toward the group he'd
been speaking with before she called him away.

The warmth of him soothed her, and she allowed
herself to breathe easier. Whatever happened next,
at least she wasn't alone.

Another memory found its way to the surface of
her mind, and she slowed her pace. "There was a
dark sedan here that night," she said, turning to point
to where the car had been. "At the end of the gravel
road, nestled up against the trees."

Knox looked in the direction she pointed, then
sent another text. "Can you tell me anything else
about the car?"

"No." She frowned. "I figured it was abandoned.
The lights were off, and I was focused on finding
Madison."

He nodded and pocketed his phone, then pulled her to him once more.

She melted into him with each slow step, trying not to think of how much she'd like to keep Knox in her life after Madison was safely home again. She wanted him as her friend, as a companion and confidant. Maybe even as her lover. She wanted Knox however she could have him, because he made her feel whole. And he'd made her feel better in the short time they'd been together than she had in a very long time, and he'd done that during two of the worst days of her life.

"Things are going to be okay," he said softly, reading her mind once more, and knowing precisely what she needed to hear.

A dark sedan appeared on the park road, several yards away, and Knox stiffened at her side. "Is that the car you saw last night?" he asked, voice tense and laced with caution.

"I—"

Before she could think or answer, the passenger window of the car rolled down and the driver's extended arm came into view, with a handgun pointed at them.

Knox was in motion before her brain could make sense of what was happening. He gripped her shoulders and pulled her sideways, nearly yanking her off her feet in the process. "Get down!" he bellowed.

She struggled to keep her feet beneath her, and the gunshots sounded as she stumbled.

Each round was fast and loud. Screams rose into the air, and for the first time since D.J. had been born, Jen hated having him on her chest. She needed to hide him, to tuck him behind her and get him out of the line of fire, but there was nothing she could do.

She wrapped her arms around her baby in the sling and pumped her legs with purpose, working to keep pace as Knox dragged them behind his nearby truck for safety. The window above them exploded, raining the broken glass over them and into their hair.

Tires squealed and an engine roared in her ringing ears as the car raced away.

In the distance, cries of emergency responders wound to life.

In her arms, a stiff and red-faced D.J. screamed and arched his back in panic.

In that moment, Jen's tears began to fall.

KNOX SETTLED JEN and D.J. into his office at the sheriff's department an hour later. His brother, Cruz, had picked them up from the carousel, after Knox and Jen had given their verbal statements. His pickup was on its way to the shop for a new window.

Meanwhile, Jen had provided a written account of the park shooting while Knox had followed up on the lead about the car. There had been a dark sedan outside Katie's house when they left too.

He watched as she played with her son, finally calmed after the awful experience. Her smile was present but false. D.J. didn't seem to notice, but Knox had learned to differentiate between the looks. The one she wore now was meant to put others at ease, usually her son. The expression was a good facsimile, but he could see the strain in her eyes and tight set of her jaw.

Jen glanced in Knox's direction, and he longed to reach for her. To comfort her and hold her. The urge was becoming impossibly difficult to deny, and he'd found himself indulging it far too often. How many times had he put his arm around her? Hugged her? Taken her hand or set a palm against her back? He had no right to do any of those things, yet she never denied him. Never stiffened or sidestepped. In fact, the opposite always happened. She relaxed into his touch, and his heart expanded further every time.

A knock on the open door drew his gaze from Jen to his brother, Cruz, leaning against the jamb.

Cruz smiled his ten-thousand-watt smile and crossed his ankles. "How's everyone holding up?" he asked, sliding his eyes from Knox to Jen and D.J.

His older brother had caught him staring at the woman in his care, and was amused. "We're good," Knox said. "Thanks for the ride earlier. I didn't realize you were still here."

Cruz shrugged. "I had a few things to follow up on." His private investigations firm kept him in regular contact with local law enforcement, so that wasn't a surprise. Still, Knox couldn't help thinking his brother appeared to have an agenda.

Jen smiled, the expression still not reaching her

eyes. "We were lucky today. Thanks for getting us out of there," she said. "The carousel is officially ruined for me. I don't care if its renovation is legendary."

Cruz grinned. "How's the little one?"

"Perfect," she said, turning her son on her lap to face him.

Cruz made a few goofy faces and sounds at D.J., before winking at Jen and heading to Knox's desk.

Knox wondered if punching his older brother in the eye might keep it from winking at Jen again, then he laughed at the ridiculous thought and sighed. Clearly, he needed more sufficient rest, and possibly some good old-fashioned Kentucky bourbon. Because he was not himself.

Cruz sat on the corner of Knox's desk, one smug foot dangling, the other planted on the ground. "Any word on the camera footage?"

"Not yet," Knox answered. He double-checked his text messages and inbox, just in case he'd missed the update. He hadn't.

"Want me to look into it?" Cruz asked. "I'm guessing you'd like to get home."

Knox nodded. "Thanks." The Jefferson County Sheriff's Department was small by any standard, but especially when compared to the sheer amount of geographical area the deputies covered. And MX-10 had been running them ragged for the past couple months. As a result, they'd been calling Cruz and his partner, their cousin Derek, in more often.

"No problem," Cruz said. "Anything else?"

Knox rubbed his throat, mind racing over the day. "Maybe," he said. "I can't be sure, but I think the sedan in the park was the same one I saw parked on the receptionist's block earlier. The one outside Katie's place had a temporary tag in the window, but I don't know if this one did," he admitted, hating that he'd missed such an important detail.

His mind had been on Jen and D.J. instead of in lawman mode. Normally, he could remain calm through anything, because he wasn't worried about getting hurt. He never had been. Maybe that was a personality defect. Maybe it was a sign of damage done to a kid who'd lost his mother too soon, or a man who'd lost too much overseas. But he'd never feared for himself, and that fact made him a better lawman. He wasn't hindered by self-concern. When push came to shove, Knox could shove hard, and take in the most minute of details while he did.

But not today. Not with Jen and D.J. in danger.

Today, his body had responded on instinct, and the only thing his mind could manage was *Not them. Please, not them.*

Cruz tented his brows. "You followed the receptionist from her place. You think the shooter followed you?"

"Maybe," he said again. Truthfully, he wasn't sure of anything anymore, and he hated the tangling of his thoughts almost as much as the fact they'd been shot at. He'd never been tailed without knowing before. And a screwup like that could've cost Jen and D.J. their lives.

Jen shifted, drawing the brothers' attention, and her gaze settled on Knox. "Did you learn anything from the folks you gave the burgers to?"

Cruz twisted on the desktop for a better look at Knox. "I almost forgot you head down there on weekends with food. What did they say? Anyone see anything?"

"Yeah," Knox said. "Actually they did, but nothing helpful. They tried though. I'll give them that. They saw a man dressed in black and carrying a gun. He wore a ski mask, so they couldn't describe his features. He was alone when they saw him, and came within a few feet of the group, gun brandished, before moving on."

Cruz made a disgusted sound. "He was probably looking for Jen's roommate, and she was hiding by the carousel. He must've found her after that."

"That's my guess," Knox said.

His brother's clear green eyes flashed. "All right then," he said, stretching onto his feet. "I brought you a loaner car and saw to it that your window will be fixed and the pickup returned to your place when it's ready. If you need anything else, give me a call." He produced a key fob from his pocket and set it on Knox's desk, then tipped his invisible hat and sauntered out the door.

Jen watched him leave, curiosity on her brow. She

turned her attention back to Knox a moment later and grinned. "Your brother is nice."

He narrowed his eyes. "Yeah." Knox loved and respected his older brother more than just about anyone on the planet, so the odd sense of jealousy that hit with her words caught him off guard. He didn't like it.

She wouldn't be the first person to prefer Cruz to Knox. Most folks did. Cruz had that effect on people, especially women. They liked his confidence, his attitude and his swagger. Knox considered himself a likable guy, but compared to Cruz, he was a surly curmudgeon.

"You look a lot alike," Jen continued. "Are you ever mistaken for twins?"

"Not since we were kids," Knox said, a smirk creeping over his face. "Once I gained two inches on him, he was mistaken for the younger brother though. I thought it was funny at the time, but the closer I get to thirty, the more appealing being the younger brother has become."

She smiled. "Were your personalities always so different?"

That observation gave him pause. Jen had only spoken to Cruz a few minutes on the ride from the park, then a few more just now. "What do you mean?" he asked, before he could think better of it. Of course she'd noticed the differences between brothers. He and Cruz were like night and day. And Jen missed very little.

"I'm not sure," she said. "He might've been putting on a show for my sake, maybe to cheer me up," she clarified. "But he seems to be a charmer in the most charismatic sense of the word."

"That's Cruz," Knox said, smiling at her careful but accurate word choices. "People love him, and he loves that people love him."

She laughed. "And what do people think about you?" she asked.

Knox felt his resting grouch face return. "I'm too serious, and I need to relax. I'm steadfast and capable, but not the brother to have around if you're looking for a lot of jokes and small talk."

Jen nodded, accepting Knox's self-description, while he tried to figure out why he'd said so much.

"I think we're done here," he said, breaking the strange, suddenly palpable tension. "If you're ready, we can grab an early dinner and head back to your place. We've completely missed lunch."

She stood and nodded. "Okay."

He took the diaper bag before she could slip it over her shoulder, then he reached for her hand.

"Knox?" she asked, turning her palm against his and lacing their fingers.

"Yeah?"

"Is it okay if you're my favorite Winchester brother?" she asked.

A careful smile lifted Knox's cheeks, and a bubble of hope expanded in his chest. "Yeah."

"Good," she said, nodding as she raised her eyes to his. "Because I prefer steadfast to small talk."

Chapter Eleven

After dinner, Jen gave D.J. a bath, then strapped him into his bouncy seat so she could take a shower. She spent a prolonged amount of time attempting to wash away the awful day. The water and baby giggles went a long way to removing her tension.

Knowing Knox Winchester was in her living room, fully capable of protecting them all, and possibly attracted to her too, sent a flutter of comfort and joy through her core. She'd seen the interest in his eyes several times, though he hadn't said a word to confirm or deny it. But their connection was so much deeper than the danger they'd been in or the case they were working. Life was easy with him at her side. The time passed too quickly and always with warmth and laughter.

She stepped into the hall several minutes later, dressed in fresh yoga pants and a T-shirt. Her towel-dried hair was twisted into a high loose bun.

Not surprisingly, Knox had cleaned up the take-out containers from their meal while she and D.J.

were busy. He'd also turned on the living room television and selected the local news station.

Jen pressed her eyes shut, sending up silent prayers for a new development on Madison's case. This was the end of the second day she'd been missing, and every hour she remained gone was an hour closer to the point where most missing persons didn't make it home.

D.J. cooed, opening Jen's eyes, and she carried on, shoulders back and chin up. She stopped at the front door to check the new locks once more. The deadbolt and knob had both been changed. She added the chain for good measure, and hoped Knox would consider staying another night or two. She doubted she'd be able to sleep otherwise.

"We're back," she announced when Knox looked up from his phone. "Sorry it took so long. You didn't have to clean up."

"I wanted to, and you should take as long as you need," he said. "Feeling any better?"

"A little." She set the bouncy seat on the floor near the couch and gave D.J. a snuggle before buckling him in once more. "Now, I just have to call off work so no one worries, and there's enough time to replace me. My next class isn't until the day after tomorrow, but I'm going to let them know what's going on, then bow out for the rest of the week." She bit her lip as a horrible thought arose. "At least I hope this will be over in a week." She grabbed her phone and dropped onto the cushion beside Knox.

His arm went easily around her. "We're going to do everything we can," he said.

She made the call with as much confidence and positivity as she could muster, despite her boss's well-intentioned questions and concern. Then disconnected with a sigh.

Knox wrapped his arm a little tighter, urging her to lean on him. "How'd you get a job teaching swim classes at the community center?" he asked. "I feel like there's a story there."

She pressed her lips together a moment, before reluctantly admitting the unconventional truth. "My dad was a swim coach until his heart attack, so I grew up in the water. Swimming is just about the only thing I'm qualified to do, and I do it pretty well."

Knox smiled. "Have you always wanted to coach like your dad?"

"No." She nearly snorted at the idea. Not that she didn't love her job. There was just so much more behind the decision to work at a pool. "I started swimming competitively before I could write my name, legibly anyway. I was five. I got a full athletic scholarship for college after high school, then I blew out my shoulder in training one day, and that was that. It didn't heal right. My times climbed. My scholarship disappeared, and I had to figure out who I was and what I wanted to do with my life if I couldn't swim."

Knox was still and quiet. Probably trying to decide what to say, so she pressed on.

"People hear about male athletes going through

things like this more often than women. It happens, but it's not quite so newsworthy. I had a hard time finding women to talk to about it, and I grew bitter. I rebelled. Pushed everyone away who I suspected might try to comfort me. I felt like a failure and wanted to wallow." She smiled. "That was all wrong, of course. I see that now, but I didn't then. Thankfully, I met Dylan before I did anything too crazy, and I gave in to the wonders of a first love. Life with him was a whirlwind. It was exciting and ever-changing. We traveled when he was on leave. Always a new town. New adventure. Then sometimes he was gone for months. It was hard not knowing where he was or if he was okay. Then one day he was just gone."

She felt her breath shudder as she exhaled. "My parents warned me against the engagement. In fairness, they were right. I barely knew him. But Dylan made me feel alive. I hadn't felt so free and peaceful outside the water in a long time. Still, they didn't approve, and they made sure I knew."

"How are you and your folks doing now?" Knox asked.

"Okay. They call about once a week and check in. They adore D.J., and wish I lived closer." She gave a short humorless laugh. "They think it isn't safe for two women and a baby to live alone."

"Is that why you haven't called to tell them what you're going through?"

Jen sighed. She dreaded their next call. Having to tell them what was happening would be awful. They'd say they told her so. They'd be terrified and her dad would probably be on a plane to collect her before she finished her story. She'd almost called them last night, when she couldn't sleep, but she knew she'd never get the words off her tongue. "They invited me to come home to Florida while they were in town for Dylan's funeral, but I wasn't ready to think about starting over again. The concept seemed too big. And I didn't want to leave Dylan. I thought I'd visit his grave every day." She gave a soft smile. "I do not."

"He wouldn't want you to," Knox said. "No one wants that for their loved ones. Would you?"

Jen rested her head against his chest, knowing he was right. "No."

She reached for Knox's hand and let herself imagine a life with him. Silly as it was. And with too many scary things happening all around them. She indulged the fantasy, and it felt like home.

KNOX PULLED JEN in close. She melted against him as always, and he appreciated the complexity of her. So strong and still so loving. He hated knowing her family was so far away when she needed them. The idea of seeing her get on a plane to Florida made him feel hollow, but at least she and D.J. would be safe there. "You really should find a way to visit."

"Yeah." She tipped her head back and cast a shy look in his direction. "Maybe the next time you have some vacation days, you can visit them with me."

Knox felt his insides twist at the thought of taking a trip with Jen, especially one so important. So he set his mind to make it happen.

"Anyway," she said with a sigh, "I've always worked at pools since then. Sometimes I coach youth leagues or teach adult lessons, but right now I specialize in Water Babies and mommy-and-me classes, because I can take D.J. with me."

Knox tipped his head to hers, resting his cheek against her crown.

"Should we call the clinic and make an appointment to speak with the doctors?" she asked, changing the subject back to the crisis at hand.

"Definitely not," he said, determined to keep her out of harm's way moving forward. "Deputies will take care of that. Abel's name was on the list at the park, and they'll figure out why. Right now, my job is to keep you and D.J. safe, and your job is to let me."

He didn't have a single guess about what the names meant or how they were related, and it was sure to make him insane. There was nothing more grating than an unanswered question.

Jen reached for his free hand and pulled it across her middle, snuggling in for comfort. She angled her body and tipped her head to look at him. "What do you think Madison was trying to tell us with that list?" she asked.

"I don't know, but the sheriff's department will figure it out," he assured.

"Then we'll hop on a plane to Florida?" she asked, her tone teasing.

"Absolutely," he agreed, trying not to think about her sweet breath blowing across his face.

She was so impossibly close. He'd barely have to move to press his mouth to hers. Her gaze dropped to his lips, and his reckless heart gave a heavy thud.

This isn't the time, he reminded himself, especially considering what he still needed to ask her.

He'd planned to talk to her as soon as she and D.J. came back from the shower, but he'd let himself get distracted, and the time was only getting later. "Before we go to Florida," he said softly, his self-control waning, "how do you feel about spending tonight at my place?"

Chapter Twelve

Jen easily agreed to spending the night at Knox's place. She hadn't cared where they stayed, as long as he was with her, and she knew D.J. would be safe. She also couldn't complain about getting more time with Knox, whom she couldn't seem to get enough of.

D.J. had fallen asleep before she'd managed to finish packing, so they'd agreed to leave after he woke. Until then, she gathered the things they might need.

"Don't worry about all the baby equipment," Knox called from the living room, where he'd volunteered to break down the portable crib for transport. "My auntie and uncle keep one of everything baby gear—related at their place for when they babysit. And their stuff gets toted around, house to house, as needed when new kids come on board."

Jen stopped folding onesies for D.J. and backed into the hallway between the bedroom and living room. "Did you say when new kids come on board?"

He flashed a crooked smile from her living room.

"My family was big by anyone's standards two years ago. Today, we could qualify as our own country."

"Winchester Country, huh?" she asked, returning to her packing. "Sounds wild."

"You have no idea."

She finished in the bedroom, then turned out the light on her way back to the living room. "I think this is everything," she said, setting the final duffel bag with the other things already stacked near her front door. She tried to imagine temporarily moving into Knox's home and failed. Squinting, she realized she hadn't asked a very important question. "Where do you live?"

Knox was a deputy sheriff. His jurisdiction covered the entire county. He might not even live in her town for all she knew, and she suddenly couldn't believe she didn't know.

"I'm about twenty minutes from here," he said. "On the outskirts between Great Falls and West Liberty. Not too far to run back for anything you forget."

That seemed acceptable, and incredibly comforting, because she wasn't sure what she'd need for an indefinite amount of time away from home. She and D.J. had never left the apartment for more than a few hours.

"Are you sure this is okay?" she asked, suddenly second-guessing his offer to move a new mom and her baby into his home. The bag in the kitchen, filled with infinite baby food jars, bottles and formula cans, was bigger than D.J.'s diaper bag, and that had his favorite blanket in it. "We're going to overrun your bachelor pad."

Knox laughed, then gave her a warm, sincere look. "I'm glad to have you both for as long as you need. I wish it wasn't under these circumstances, but I wouldn't trust many other people to keep you safe, so this works out just fine. Besides," he added, watching her over the half-collapsed crib between them, "I'm looking forward to getting to know you better."

Her cheeks warmed, and so did her heart. "Me too," she said. "You're my hero, Knox Winchester."

He chuckled. "Glad to hear it. I don't plan to have my title revoked anytime soon, so I'd better get back to work." He rooted in her little pink-and-black tool kit for something to use on the portable crib.

She'd purchased the item at a garage sale when she was pregnant, and it was a great crib, but it was old and testy. Not always easy to set up or tear down. She'd decided months ago it was easiest to leave it set up at all times, and just drag it from room to room as needed. Madison sometimes helped her carry it with D.J. playing inside. If it hadn't been for Madison, Jen probably would've moved home to Florida with her parents. Her life would be completely different. And Madison would still be in Missouri. And she would be safe.

Knox left the crib and moved across the space in her direction. "You okay?"

She nodded, but struggled to meet his eye, hoping he wouldn't see the wash of emotion on her face.

"Hey," he said, stopping a few feet in front of her. "I've been thinking. You've had a lot happen to you since we originally met. You lost Dylan. Had a baby. Your family's halfway across the country." He waited for her to meet his gaze before going on. "Aside from this mess with Madison, how are you really doing?"

Jen bit her lip and forced herself to hold his eye contact. No one had asked her how she was doing, not really, in a very long time. "I'm okay," she said, and unlike a long period of time during and immediately after her pregnancy, she meant it.

"Things must be hard without Dylan," Knox said.

She shrugged. "Sure. I was lucky to have him in my life, even if it was only for a little while. He was easy to love and exactly what I'd needed while I figured out who I was or wanted to be without swim."

Knox nodded, crossing his arms and resting his backside against her counter, intently focused, as if her words were the most important ones in the world. And he needed to concentrate. "And who are you now?"

She smiled. "I'm strong," she said. "In different ways than I was before. New ways. More ways. I'm capable. I'm happy, and I'm content. D.J. is hands down the best thing that has ever happened to me, and being with him fulfills me in ways I never could've imagined before. I wasn't ready for a pregnancy, or for motherhood, but I wouldn't trade a moment of it for anything. I don't feel like I'm searching anymore. I feel like I am who I was meant to be, and I like this person."

Knox scanned her face with his gaze, examining her, evaluating her. And she couldn't help wondering what he saw there.

"What?" she asked finally.

He shook his head. "I think you're incredible."

"I try," she said, offering a shy smile. "There wasn't any choice once I learned I was pregnant. D.J. needed a mother."

Knox nodded. "What do you need?" he asked, still watching her with careful, evaluating eyes.

She gave a soft laugh. "I just need him to be safe," she said. "Anything other than that is icing."

"So, tell me about the icing."

Jen smiled. "I'd like to find a partner in this life someday. Someone to grow old with, to fight with, to make up with." She paused, thinking carefully about what she'd say next. "I want someone I know will always have my back, whatever comes. And I want a role model for D.J. A father figure who can do the things with him that Dylan can't. I think Dylan would want that too."

Knox nodded. "He would."

"But not another military man," she said, the words popping free without much thought. "No more men who live for exciting, special-ops, dangerous missions in far-off places. That was for a younger, child-free me."

Knox frowned deeply, his enviable light and good humor gone. "Explain, please."

She frowned back at him, ruffled by his reaction to her truth. "Because I've changed." She motioned to D.J., snoozing in his bouncy seat. "Everything has changed."

"And you wouldn't want a partner whose life was regularly in danger," he said, evidently forlorn at the thought.

"No." She shook her head. "Not that. It's more about the deployment. Because I'd really like to find someone who will always be around." She smiled, a small self-deprecating smile. "I've gotten selfish in the last year. I want a man who'd be here for me and D.J., every day. A man who wants to be here. Day in and day out, for the good and the bad. I want a full-time partner in my life."

"So, you wouldn't mind a partner who had a dangerous job?" Knox asked. "Even if he worked long hours and his shifts varied?"

She smiled, and heat flooded her once more. "Not as long as he showed up for D.J. and me when it counted."

His frown eased. "So, a standard lawman, for example," he said, eyes twinkling, "would be acceptable, but not a marshal or agent who might have to go undercover for long stints of time."

"Correct. I want the whole boring, wonderful, run-of-the-mill family experience."

"Like a man who coaches D.J.'s Little League and attends Scout meetings."

"I'll lead the Scout meetings," she said. "Obviously."

"And the swim classes?" Knox asked, his smile growing as he spoke.

"We can split those."

"Got it," Knox said, nodding. "And how will you know when you've found this guy?"

A wicked smile twisted her lips, and she shot a teasing look at her friend. "Because he'll be all-in from the start, and he'll want more than just my body."

He pressed a hand to his chest and groaned. "Let's keep it clean, Jordan. I'm still trying not to picture you in a swimsuit."

She laughed, and he went back to the crib. "Do you need some help?" she asked, following in his wake.

"Absolutely." He waved to the mostly flattened piece of baby equipment. "Unless I'm missing something, this seems to be completely stuck."

As she suspected. "Screwdriver," she said, offering him her open palm.

"Flathead or Phillips?" he asked, not bothering to lecture her on the obvious fact there wasn't anything on the crib in need of that particular tool.

"Either."

Knox handed her a flathead. "All right. Show me what I'm missing."

She felt along the padded blue cover for the rusty

joint hidden just out of sight, then whacked it with the handle of her screwdriver, and the side swung down.

Knox clapped slowly in appreciation. "Nice."

She returned the screwdriver, and their fingers touched. Heat raced up her arm to her chest, and she stepped closer on instinct, eagerly seeking more.

Knox's gaze darkened, and his hands settled on the curves of her waist. "Thank you for your help," he said, tugging her closer still. "I was ready to chuck the whole thing out the window, but you knew just what to do."

"It's what I do," she said. "I'm a problem-solver."

He grinned.

She looked up at him, and the heat pooling in her core seemed to be reflected in his eyes. She'd nearly kissed him on the couch, when their mouths had been so close she could feel his breath on her face. Something had stopped her then, making her think it wasn't the right time. But she was more positive with every exchange that Knox was a man worth kissing. He was a man worth holding on to.

His broad palms skimmed her back. One set of strong fingers gripped her at the waist, pulling her against him, while the other hand glided up her spine to cradle her neck.

Her back arched in response, and her breath caught as his gaze lowered to her parted lips.

D.J.'s sudden cry sent a bout of nervous laughter from her lips, and Jen spun on her heels to collect her whimpering son. He never woke upset, and her heart clenched at the probability the day had left a dark spot on his psyche somehow. She cooed and rocked him, holding him close as she dared a look at Knox.

He leaned against the armchair a few feet away, unmoving. His eyes danced as he rubbed a forefinger across his lightly stubbled chin. A playful smile curved his lips.

She considered a number of silly comments about the way she'd jumped, as if she was a child who'd been caught doing something wrong.

But Knox's smile fell before she could find the right words, and he grabbed the television remote from the coffee table. "Jen," he said, raising the volume on a newscast as he moved in close to her side.

A breaking-news report had begun, complete with a red ribbon stretched across the bottom of her screen. The words *Death in Downtown* curled icy fingers into her gut.

The pretty blonde reporter tossed her hair and feigned sadness at the camera. "...sad to report a fatal accident at a busy downtown intersection earlier today. Eyewitnesses say that the driver ran a stoplight at the intersection of Jefferson and First Avenue. The car was then struck by a city utilities truck and forced into oncoming traffic, where it rolled several times before colliding with a tree. The car's driver, and only passenger, was ejected and pronounced dead at the scene. She is the only known fatality at this time."

Jen stared breathlessly at the remains of a small red hatchback on her television screen. Undeniably, the receptionist's car.

Chapter Thirteen

Jen wobbled and reached for the island to steady herself. The red hatchback they'd followed from Katie's home through downtown looked nearly annihilated on screen. A mass of emergency responders filled the area, and roadblocks were set up to control traffic and onlookers.

"She's dead," Jen whispered, her stomach knotting and her breaths coming in short shallow pants. "I feel sick."

Knox moved to her side and lowered before her, enough to catch her eyes. "May I hold D.J.?" he asked, gently taking the baby from her arms. "Thank you. Now, why don't you have a seat on the couch? I'll get you some water."

Jen let him lead her to the sofa, then she pulled her legs to her chest while she watched the onscreen horrors unfold. "The accident happened earlier today," she said. "How long do you think it was after we lost track of her? Did the cruiser ever catch up?"

Knox returned with a cold bottle of water and

passed it to her. "I'll send a text and see what happened."

She dragged her gaze from the television to Knox, who was confidently comforting her son in one arm and texting with his free hand. His expression was impossibly calm despite the unthinkable turn of events.

Her thoughts were muddled as memories of the clinic's receptionist flickered in and out through the shock. The photographs on Katie's mantel came to mind. "Her poor son," she whispered, nausea rising at the memory.

"Drink," Knox said, motioning to the bottle in her hand. "I think it's time we get moving as soon as you're feeling steady." His gaze drifted to the television. "I want to get you both back to my place."

Jen's intuition spiked. The look on Knox's face said everything he hadn't. "You don't think the crash was an accident," she said.

"I don't know." Knox locked his eyes on hers. "The timing is questionable, and I can't help wondering if you're in more danger than I imagined. I'll feel safer once we're at my place." He cuddled D.J. close and tipped his cheek against her son's hair.

She nodded, taking another long drag on the bottle before pushing onto her feet. She wouldn't keep D.J. anywhere potentially unsafe. "So there isn't any chance that this was a horrible coincidence?"

"Few things ever are."

Jen stuffed her feet into waiting sneakers, then went to grab her purse, phone and keys.

Knox's phone dinged, and he swiped a thumb across the screen to read the message. "I've got confirmation that Katie's accident is being considered as connected to Madison's disappearance." He looked up with a nod. "That's good news. It means Madison's picture will be posted on local and state news and social-media channels. A whole lot more people will know she's missing, and our chances of finding her improve."

Her heart hammered, and hope rose in her chest.

The news reporter's voice drew Jen's attention back to the screen. "…this afternoon's fatal downtown traffic accident may not have been an accident, after all. Reports of a severed brake line have begun to roll in, but the Jefferson County Sheriff's Department is refusing to comment."

Jen's breath caught as the screen went dark.

Beside her, Knox lowered the remote to the counter and fixed her with a stare. "Ready?"

She nodded, and they gathered the things she'd stacked near the front door.

Of course Knox had predicted Katie's crash wasn't an accident. It was his job to get ahead of things, to be astute and cautious. Jen wondered what else he'd been right about. The pills hidden in her bathroom came to mind. "This is about the baggie of MX-10. Isn't it? You were right about that too."

Knox held the door while she passed. He locked up

behind them, then ushered her quickly to his truck. "I was wrong when I thought Madison was using those pills," he said when they were safely in his truck. "I can see I misjudged her now, but I'm willing to bet she learned something about MX-10 that she shouldn't know, and Katie knew it too."

THEY RODE IN silence until eventually arriving at a small brick ranch with black roof and shutters. The lot was sizable with mature trees and a tire swing in the massive oak out front.

The home was cute and quaint, situated at the end of a long gravel lane off the county road. Jen took in the property details, gently illuminated by landscape and security lighting. Black mulch beds were polkadotted with neatly trimmed shrubs and brightly colored flowers.

A large garden stone, situated near the porch steps, had two neatly scripted words across its center.

Welcome Home.

Knox climbed out and opened the extended cab's door to collect D.J.

Jen fixed her eyes on the inviting front porch, large welcome mat and quaint red rocking chair. A matching red barn sat several yards away in the lush green grass. She smiled at the little structure. He probably kept a lawn tractor and gardening tools inside.

Clearly, when Knox Winchester wasn't being a deputy sheriff, or her personal hero, he was a regular guy with an adorable home and a plot of land he tended.

He strode onto the porch with her baby in one arm and several bags looped over his shoulders. "You okay?" he asked, casting a look her way.

"Yeah." She followed, warmed by the unexpectedly domestic scene. She hadn't given much thought to where Knox lived, but she also hadn't expected this. She would've assumed he had an apartment like hers, if she'd expected anything at all. A single-man lair of some sort. Either utterly messy or cold and efficient due to his demanding job. The home and land before her were something else entirely.

He ushered her inside from his place on the porch, an inviting smile on his lips, and her baby snuggled contentedly against his chest. She imagined the scene unfolding a dozen times, each with Knox and D.J. growing older. Then flashes of Knox teaching D.J. to ride a bike on the gravel lane, pushing him in the tire swing under the oak tree and playing catch on the large front lawn. Her eyes and nose stung with unexpected emotion, and she covered it with a yawn.

The ideas were silly and impossible. A result of her strung-out state. And they were also more than she'd dared to dream of since losing Dylan.

"Come on. I'll give you the ten-cent tour," Knox said, as she passed him in the doorframe. "Think you're ready?"

"Yes." The answer was honest, and she knew it covered much more than a tour.

KNOX ROSE WITH the sun the next morning. He'd barely slept and was eager to get started on a new day. Hopefully, the next twenty-four hours would bring authorities closer to finding Jen's missing roommate than yesterday had. His heart had gone out to Katie, her family and especially her poor son. If only she'd clued Knox in to whatever was going on with Madison and what she knew about the MX-10, maybe Knox could've saved her. He'd run through the possibilities a thousand times. She might still have run, might not have let him take her into custody. Heck, depending on what she'd said, he might not have offered to take her anywhere, and she still would've gotten into an unsafe car the next time she left home.

He stretched a T-shirt over his head and pressed the heels of his hands against his eyes, hating the utter helplessness he felt. And despising the creators and distributors of a street drug that was taking far too many lives.

Knox shuffled into the hallway, ready for a pot of coffee and some food, when the sound of running water slowed his pace. The bathroom door was closed, but the soft scents of steam and soap curled into the hall. Apparently, Jen was already awake too. Hopefully, she'd managed more sleep than he had.

A squeaky baby sound drew Knox's attention to the portable crib he and Jen had set up inside her room. D.J.'s legs were in the air. One sock on and one bare foot grasped in his chubby hands.

Knox snorted and changed directions. He crept

into the guest room for a look at the little brown-haired butterball.

D.J. squeaked again at the sight of him, and Knox chuckled. D.J. released his foot and stretched his arms into the air.

"Well, good morning to you too," Knox said, enchanted by the wide toothless smile. He lifted the pint-sized bundle from the crib and nestled him against his side. His diaper made the dry papery sound of a newly installed model, and his pajamas had been swapped for some kind of kiddie-sized baseball uniform. The look made Knox laugh. "I guess you were awake before your mama got into the shower, and she prepared you for the day first." That seemed in keeping with what Knox knew about her. Always putting others first. Making her son priority one. Knox had nothing but respect for that.

He turned for the door and carried D.J. into the kitchen. "I hope your mama won't mind if you help me with breakfast," he said, propping the baby on one hip while he set the coffee to brew. Next, he buckled D.J. into the portable high chair Jen had packed and scanned the counter full of baby bottles and foods. "I guess you get a bottle every morning?" he asked D.J. "It's made with water and some of that powdered formula, right? What about food?" He went back to the counter and lifted the hoard of foodstuffs. "Cereal?" He shook the box, then a few flakes onto his palm. "You eat this mixed with water?" Knox frowned and stuck out his tongue.

D.J. laughed.

Knox prepared a bottle, following the instructions on the formula can, then he started on a meal for the grown folks while the kid enjoyed his drink.

Once the oven had preheated, Knox placed a frozen casserole inside to bake. Next, he selected a knife and chopping board, along with several pieces of fresh fruit.

The pipes of his old home shuddered as he sipped his steaming coffee, signaling the end of Jen's shower. Knox did what he could to push images of her bare skin from his mind with excruciating effort. Knowing she was naked on the other side of the shared kitchen and bathroom wall was more temptation than his suddenly active imagination could handle.

D.J. patted his high chair tray, drawing Knox back to the moment.

He smiled at the thought of endless mornings like this one. Mornings when Jen and D.J. were here by choice and not as a matter of safety. He recalled her words about wanting a life partner, and someone who'd be a father to D.J. in Dylan's absence.

Knox's chest tightened as he let himself imagine filling both those roles. What would it be like if Jen and D.J. were his, and he belonged to them as well? Fishing trips with his family, and D.J. in the camp chair beside his. Laughs over shared meals, and late nights of showing Jen exactly how much she meant to him.

Soft footfalls drew his attention to the hallway beside the kitchen.

Jen appeared in black stretchy pants and a crimson top that exposed a sliver of skin when she raised a hand in greeting. Her hair was up again, and miraculously dry, somehow having eluded the shower. "Sorry," she said, looking unexplainably guilty. "I didn't mean to take so long. Normally, D.J. doesn't mind. I hope he wasn't crying. I can usually hear his whimpers from a mile away."

Knox poured a second mug of coffee, then lifted it to her in offering. "He's in a great mood. When I saw he was awake, I brought him out here with me for some man time."

She rolled her eyes and smiled. "How's that going?"

"Pretty well," he said. "I taught him to change the oil in your car before that bottle."

Her smile widened.

"Hungry?" he asked. His eyes skimmed her flushed pink skin, unbidden, and he jerked them back to her happy face.

"Starving." She smiled as she made her way to D.J. "Thank you for making him a bottle."

"It's no problem. I've got a casserole in the oven for us, and I'm making a fruit salad. I wasn't home for the last day or two, so I need to use this up."

Jen returned to Knox's side and selected a plastic bowl and spoon from D.J.'s meal supplies. "You don't have to do all this. Babysitting. Cooking." She waved the airplane-shaped spoon between them. "Letting us stay here is already too much."

He shot her a bland expression. "Please. My auntie keeps my freezer filled with more casseroles than one man could ever eat. She loves us with food, and clearly thinks I'm helpless."

"And the fruit?" she asked, resting her backside against the counter to his right.

"I like fruit."

She laughed, and the tightness in his heart unfurled.

He watched as she whipped up some mush with the baby cereal flakes, then opened a tiny jar of bananas and carried the meal to D.J.

Jen kissed her baby's head before taking the seat beside his chair. "I think it's sweet your auntie makes you casseroles. It shows how much she loves you. How many Winchester bachelors are there?"

He thought about all the weddings and engagement parties he'd been invited to in the last year and grimaced. He'd never even taken a date. Truthfully, no one had held his attention in a very long time. And no one had ever captivated him like Jen. "Only one," he said over his shoulder, lifting one hand as he pulled the casserole from the oven with the other. "Technically, I suppose there are two. We have another unmarried cousin, Nash, in Louisville, but he's too far away for Auntie to deliver meals or worry about. Plus, Nash's folks are in town with him, so she doesn't have to worry about the poor, helpless veteran and US marshal."

Jen spooned D.J.'s breakfast into his open birdy mouth. "How old is he?"

"Cruz's age," Knox said. "Maybe a year older."

Her brows furrowed, and her lips parted as she delivered each bite to her son.

Knox grinned as he plated their breakfasts and ferried everything to the little table.

D.J. bounced in his seat, legs kicking and arms flung wide, gobbling up the meal as quickly as his mama could provide it. His wide brown eyes tracked Knox's arrival.

Jen glanced up as Knox sat. "I fell asleep thinking about Florida last night," she said. "You were right. It's time I take D.J. to see my family. As soon as I know Madison is okay."

He smiled, glad for her sake and her family's, but feeling the loss at the mention of her leaving. "I think that's good," he said. "After all this, you'll need some time to recuperate. I'll keep a close eye on Madison so you won't have to worry."

Her brows rose. "You'll have to get someone else to do that," she said, scraping D.J.'s cereal bowl with a little plastic spoon. "You're coming with us."

A wide grin spread across Knox's lips and his heart gave a heavy kick.

The moment was cut short by his doorbell.

Whoever was out there had the world's worst timing, and he was nearly positive it was his brother.

Knox swiped the screen on his phone to life and checked the front porch camera.

Cruz waved cheerfully back.

Jen laughed, apparently spotting the image. "Is that Cruz?"

Knox stood with a sigh. "Welcome to Winchester Country, where you're always fed and rarely alone for long."

Chapter Fourteen

Cruz waltzed in, as carefree and attention commanding as usual.

Knox checked the driveway for signs of additional Winchesters before locking the door behind him, because his family typically traveled in packs. Satisfied his brother was alone, he followed him to the kitchen.

"Mornin', Jordans," Cruz said, waving to Jen on his way to make silly faces at D.J.

"Good morning," Jen replied, glancing at Knox with a grin.

"Breakfast sure smells good," Cruz noted, taking a seat beside the high chair. "I've been up since before dawn. Barely had more than coffee." He patted the flat stomach he was eternally proud of, then shook a monkey-shaped teether for D.J.

Knox rolled his eyes, already arranging a fresh plate for the interloper. He watched Jen for her reaction. She wasn't part of the family now, but if there was hope of her sticking around long-term, she'd have to deal with his family's nosy, pushy, loving but ever-present ways.

"Were you just in the neighborhood?" Jen asked, smiling as he entertained her baby.

"Just checking in," Cruz said.

Knox ferried the full plate to his brother.

Cruz straightened, abandoning the teether at the sight of fresh fruit salad and their auntie's casserole. "You always know exactly what I need."

"You literally told me you hadn't eaten," Knox countered, taking his seat at the table.

Jen laughed softly as Cruz dug in. Her soft, warm expression at the men's exchange spread across the space to his heart.

"Anything new on the case?" Knox asked, redirecting his attention to Cruz. "My phone's been oddly quiet since last night."

Cruz shook his head. "Not much. I stopped by the sheriff's department to deliver some findings on another case this morning, then asked around about the car accident and Madison while I was there. Mechanics confirmed the car was sabotaged. There was a clear slice to the brake line, nothing that would likely happen in the course of natural use or wear and tear. Also some damage to the steering column. Together, the issues would've made it tough to steer and impossible to slow down by the time she reached the fatal intersection."

Jen set her fork aside with a clatter. "Her driving

was exponentially erratic as we followed. I thought she was just getting more upset."

Cruz bobbed his head. "That was probably true too."

Jen cringed, and Knox stifled the urge to cover her hand with his.

"I'm headed over to the clinic from here," Cruz said. "A couple deputies are planning to conduct interviews today. I figured I'd hang around, see who comes and goes. Stake the place out. Pose as a patient. Maybe overhear something of use."

Knox nodded. "I like that idea. Any chance Derek has time to get in on this?"

"He's busy." Cruz smiled. "Taking a look around Katie's house as we speak." Cruz stuffed another forkful of food into his mouth.

"Who's Derek?" Jen asked.

"My partner," Cruz said, as Knox answered, "Our cousin."

"He's a bit of a snoop and a fantastic lock-picker," Cruz added, sounding proud as usual.

Knox offered his usual, wholly ignored, warning look.

Cruz and Derek had been known to, on occasion, overlook what was legal in favor of what was helpful, especially when lives were in danger.

"A lock-picker?" Jen asked, her face scrunched in distaste, or confusion, Knox wasn't sure. "You mean he's breaking into Katie's house?" She flicked her gaze to Knox for an explanation.

Cruz waved his fork dismissively. "No. He's looking for clues about who would've hurt her and taken Madison. Nothing messy or invasive. Derek's quick and thorough. He'll be in and out without a trace. Anything he finds useful, he'll share with the sheriff's department immediately."

Knox pinned him with an unamused stare. "And how will he claim to have gotten wind of this potentially useful information this time? Considering the home owner is dead."

Cruz grinned. "Why don't we jump off that bridge when we come to it?" he suggested, mixing metaphors and tossing in a wink for good measure. "I'm sure he'll tell them the honest truth. The door was unlocked when he went inside."

"After he picked the lock," Knox said.

Cruz turned a pained expression on Jen, whose smile had returned at the increase of brotherly banter. "Knox is a fantastic lawman."

"He is," she agreed, flashing him a bright, warm smile.

"He can't always condone our actions," Cruz said, "but never complains about our respectfully gained results."

"Helpful and lawful aren't the same things," Knox said.

"Are you going to turn him in?" Cruz challenged, ending the conversation his usual way.

Knox rubbed a heavy hand over his face. "I'm on vacation."

"You would've made a great private eye." Cruz turned his face toward D.J. before Knox could work up an effective frown.

"I make a great deputy," he countered. "I hope someone is interviewing Katie's ex." And that the ex wasn't involved in her murder, or with MX-10. If her son's father went to jail, it would leave the child parentless, something no kid deserved.

"I'm sure they've got that covered," Cruz said. "You badge-types are always on the ball. Speaking of, I hear the autopsy will be today. That's fast. So this case was clearly made a priority."

Jen tensed, and Knox didn't have to ask to know what she was thinking. The words were practically written on her face. Her roommate was missing and likely in the hands of the same person or people who'd arranged Katie's death. This case was absolutely a priority.

"What are they looking for in the autopsy?" she asked.

Cruz flicked his gaze to Knox, then back. "MX-10, I'd imagine."

Knox rested his elbows on the table and clasped his hands. "Katie mentioned being in trouble before. If she has old ties to the drug community, it's possible she fell victim to the new and expanding web these pills are creating."

Jen stood with her plate and carried a half-eaten breakfast to the sink. "I'd still like to know the purpose of the list on the wall at the park," she said softly.

"Madison's name was on there, and I think she left us that message for a reason. She could've been running, or hiding, or doing anything other than scratching a random stack of names on a weathered piece of plywood, but that was how she spent her time before being dragged away. I want to know why."

The quiver in her voice pulled Knox from his chair. The look in her eyes towed him across the room to her side. "I'm sure the sheriff's department is working on that too," he said. "If the doctors are being interviewed today, then there should at least be some speculation about those names soon, especially considering Abel was one of them."

"Do you think that could be a coincidence?" Jen asked. "There are lots of people named Abel in the world."

Knox could see the true questions behind her words. *What if this is another dead end? What if the one tangible clue we have is useless?* He fixed her with his most reassuring gaze. "Anything is possible, but I don't believe in coincidences. How many people does Madison know by that name?" Knox asked, stepping carefully closer. "How many do you? Other than this doctor, I don't know any, and his name was right beneath hers on that list, separated by a single line. The deputies know that's significant, and they will figure it out." He waited for Jen to lift her gaze to his. "We will find her," he promised.

Jen nodded, and the small rapid movements sent

a cascade of tears over her cheeks. Then she stepped forward and hugged him.

Knox's arms went easily around her, and the collision of emotions that followed was nearly enough to wipe him off his feet. His heart had been broken at the sight of her tears, but the rush of joy that came with her embrace, and the fierce urge to protect her, and D.J., whatever the cost, was almost more than he could bear. Definitely, unlike anything he'd ever experienced. This wasn't their first hug, but it felt like an important one, and he held her a little more tightly because of it, like the treasure she truly was.

When the time was right, he would tell her how he felt and hope like crazy she felt the same way.

Cruz sauntered past them with an empty plate and a smile. His cool green gaze caught on Knox's and his brows raised. A small teasing smile played on his lips, but he kept whatever he was thinking to himself. Wisely.

Cruz had recently fallen for a woman he was protecting, and it had altered his world irrevocably. Knox wouldn't have believed it was possible to see his big brother so wholly taken by one woman, but there wasn't any denying the truth when they were together. And he practically worshipped the baby growing inside her. Couple those facts with his nosy nature and there was little doubt he already knew what Knox was thinking.

Jen slowly eased her grip, probably feeling their guest's entertained stare.

"Well," Cruz said, clasping his hands before him and rearranging his features to hide the knowing look he'd given his brother. "Thank you both for a delicious meal. I'm going to see what I can overhear at the clinic and report back when I have something worth bothering y'all."

Jen stepped away, wrapping her arms around her middle.

Knox felt her absence instantly and deeply.

"I appreciate what you're doing more than you can know," she said.

Cruz nodded, a rare expression of sincerity replacing his ever-present smile. "Don't mention it," he said. "This is what we do. I know it's not easy in your position, but try to rest and relax. You're in good hands." He cast a teasing look at Knox. "Figuratively and literally."

"Get out," Knox said, pointing to the door.

Cruz went with a laugh, then stopped in the threshold. "I mean it about the rest," he called back. The familiar glint had returned to his eye. "Sleep while you can. Auntie Rosa and Uncle Hank got wind there's a baby here last night, and I'm honestly in shock they didn't beat me to your door this morning."

Knox wrapped an arm around Jen's shoulders and pulled her back to his side.

She looked up at him, a bit of confusion on her brow, clearly not understanding the gravity of Cruz's statement. "What?"

"I'm pretty good with bad guys," Knox said, "but

I'm not sure I can protect you properly from my family."

Cruz's laughter trailed him to his Jeep.

Chapter Fifteen

Jen laughed when Knox's auntie and uncle arrived only minutes after Cruz departed, proving the brothers right. They only stayed long enough to say the family cabin was clean and the fridge was full in case they needed it. Then they hugged Jen and fawned gratuitously over D.J., before hurrying off to look after a grandchild so their son and his wife could spend the day alone.

His auntie promised repeatedly to be back soon, while her husband towed her toward their truck.

Jen requested a quick trip to her apartment after mention of a cabin. Thankfully, Knox had agreed. Packing for a few days at Knox's house had been one thing. Packing for a potential stay at a mountain-top cabin was something else completely. If things came to that, she wouldn't be able to pop over to her place and pick up anything she forgot, or even make a quick trip to the store if something ran out. In fact, Rosa had declared the cabin remote, and advised that internet access would require a cell phone hot spot. Worse, cell service was spotty.

For now, Jen rubbed her forehead and struggled to think of everything she and D.J. could possibly need, while reminding herself not to worry. She was an excellent planner, and they were in good hands with Knox.

The memory of his aunt's and uncle's warm smiles and tight hugs slipped sweetly back to mind. The way they'd cooed at D.J. had swelled her heart and strengthened her resolve to see her parents as soon as possible. D.J. deserved to have as much love in his life as possible, and she didn't want him to miss out on his grandparents for a minute longer than necessary.

Knox's auntie Rosa had cupped Jen's cheeks with gentle care and promised they'd get to know one another soon. It'd seemed a simple, friendly thing to say on the surface, but Jen had wondered about the way the woman had looked at Knox before she'd made the declaration. As if she might've seen something in him to suggest he'd want Jen and D.J. around when this was over. She'd no doubt seen that in Jen. And the possibility he felt the same way warmed her from the inside out. In fact, staying in Knox's life permanently, or as long as fate would allow, was a fantasy she'd indulged many times over the last couple of days.

The knob on her front door turned, and she smiled as Knox stepped inside and pocketed the key to her new locks. "Anything else?" he asked.

"Just these toys, and a couple of my favorite

books," she said. "And I want to bring along a few things from the medicine cabinet. Just in case."

On that note, she headed to the bathroom in search of D.J.'s thermometer and infant Tylenol. If her baby got sick while they were hiding out, she needed to be prepared. And if her over-the-counter pain and fever reducers didn't help, she was hauling him off that mountain and straight to his pediatrician. Period.

Knox followed her as far as the bathroom doorway. "Good thinking," he said. "The cabin has a fully stocked first aid supply for adults, but I don't think anyone's gotten around to adding the basics for kids. I shouldn't be surprised you're the one to think of it."

She smirked at his reference to her preparedness. Planning ahead was a basic personality trait of hers that had been exacerbated by fear and uncertainty following Dylan's death. She had no idea what was coming on any given day, but she'd learned that preparing for everything she could think of helped her feel more in control, and when she had the things she or D.J. needed at the exact moment one of them needed it, she felt like she could handle anything else that came their way.

She paused to run mentally through their days, thinking of all the things she and D.J. used and needed. "My mail." She always brought the mail up on her way in from work, and it filled the small box quickly, thanks to an abundance of advertisements and junk correspondence no one wanted. "There isn't any time to ask the post office to hold it. Maybe Mrs.

Hancock will?" Her building manager had been so
kind and helpful already. Maybe she wouldn't mind
checking Jen's mailbox and holding the contents until
Jen returned, or shoving it under her apartment door.

"Do you want me to check with her while you
finish up here?" Knox asked. "I'd planned to touch
base with her before we left anyway. I want her to
contact the sheriff's department if she notices anyone hanging around the building or otherwise behav-
ing suspiciously."

"Okay," Jen said. She handed him the small pouch
of infant medicines and a thermometer. "Will you put
this with the last bag on the island?"

"I'll take it all to the truck and be back in a minute," he said, curling long capable fingers around
the bag.

She walked him to the door and turned the deadbolt behind him, the way she had two other times
already.

D.J.'s soft snores rose from the living room, where
he'd fallen asleep in his swing. Enjoying his last ride,
for a while anyway, to its fullest.

Jen's contented smile fell as she recalled the reason she and D.J. weren't staying at the apartment. It
wasn't just that they could be in danger; it was that
Madison already was in danger. The resurfaced memory of her roommate's absence hit like a fist to her
gut, as it did every time the thought came to mind.
The possibility that whoever had taken Madison from
the park had hurt her, or worse, was a near-constant

terror, and each time she forgot about it, if for only a few minutes, a shameful guilt followed. Jen and D.J. had the Winchesters to comfort and protect them. Madison, wherever she was, had no one.

Thoughts of Jen's time with D.J. and Knox at the coffee shop returned to mind next. They'd been retracing Madison's steps, and Coffee Cat had told them about a notebook Madison kept. Jen hadn't had time to look for them earlier, but there was plenty of time now.

Jen hurried into Madison's room and scanned the space for anything she might've carried around and written on. News of Katie's car accident had redirected and scrambled Jen's thoughts the last time she was home, but suddenly the notebook was all she could think about. Figuring out what Madison had been writing down could be the piece of information the local sheriff's office needed to locate her and stop the criminal who'd taken her from hurting anyone else.

A single hardcover journal lay on Madison's desk beside her bed. A delicate imprint of blue waves stretched across the bottom and a yellow sun graced the top. Jen flipped the book open, then thumbed through it quickly, in search of notes or doodles.

The pages were thin and tinted the colors of a sunset. Each was neatly lined in black without a single other marking.

Jen fanned through the pages twice for good measure, then set the book aside and opened Madison's desk drawer.

A pile of spiral notebooks was stacked inside.

She removed them one by one to discover that, unlike the desktop journal, every page of every notebook was filled with writing. There were personal notes to Bob, before and after his death. Diary entries. Lists of things to do before she died. Poetry about how easily loved ones can disappear.

Jen groaned at the unpleasant notion of reading her best friend's private thoughts and letters to her fallen husband, but there wasn't any other way. And it could take hours to figure out which notebook was the one she carried regularly to the café, or if it was even in this pile. So she lifted the stack onto the desktop. "Looks like you're all coming with me," she whispered. Luckily, she had a partner to help evaluate every word, note and tittle.

She raised her eyes to the mirror hung above the desk and sighed. An image of Madison with her arms around Jen and D.J., only hours after he was born, had been taped to the gilded frame. She plucked the photo away and tucked it into her back pocket. If she also brought a magnet, she could stick the image to Knox's refrigerator door and see it anytime she needed a boost.

She turned for the hallway when a sound, like the breaking of glass, froze her temporarily in place. Her heart jerked into a sprint as her mind worked to make sense of the noise.

Her apartment door was locked, and she was alone in the space, with a sleeping infant who certainly didn't break anything. Could Knox have returned and she hadn't heard him? Could the sound have come from outside?

She stepped into the hallway, instincts on high alert, and cell phone at the ready, listening for the sound to repeat.

"Knox?" she called, moving slowly along the corridor, eyes locked on D.J., snoozing soundly in his swing.

Silence gonged in the apartment, and she wondered briefly if she'd imagined the whole thing.

The creak of a floorboard assured her she hadn't.

Her steps faltered as her view of D.J. became suddenly interrupted by a broad figure dressed in black.

Jen opened her mouth to scream, but the intruder raised his handgun and stopped her.

Across the room, a breeze blew in through the open window, and she recalled the sound of breaking glass. She'd doubted herself, and she shouldn't have. She should've called Knox immediately, but it was too late now.

The man pointed to the window, unspeaking. His cold dark eyes raged behind the black ski mask. His tall frame was tense. Edgy.

Because he knew, Jen realized, that his time was limited, and Knox would be back soon. He'd probably been watching her apartment, waiting for the opportunity to move on her.

She wasn't sure if that awareness made her safer, or put her more at risk. *A man with a gun was dangerous.* But a nervous man with a gun seemed significantly worse.

Her mind raced to assess the situation.

She couldn't go out the window and leave D.J. alone in the apartment.

And she absolutely couldn't take him with her.

The intruder grabbed her shoulder and shoved her toward the window. He still hadn't spoken, and she wondered why. Did he think she'd recognize his voice? Or that speaking would wake the baby? And if he was worried about making too much noise, would he really use the gun?

Her gaze caught on D.J. as she bumped against the edge of the couch. "My baby," she whispered, a risky idea forming in her mind. "Please," she begged, spinning to face the gunman, hands raised in surrender. "Don't do this. My baby will be alone. His father died in Afghanistan before he was born. I'm all he's got." She didn't have to fake the tears that rolled freely from her eyes. And she didn't try to stop them. Her neck and cheeks heated. Her stomach coiled.

The man released a low guttural sound, then lunged at her, likely planning to throw her out the window if necessary.

She dodged the incoming blow, but pretended to fall. "Please!" She roared the word this time, letting her emotions take over, and not attempting to get up or run.

If she was lucky, the man would leave rather than be caught by Knox.

"Don't hurt my baby!" She sobbed, bowing her head and pressing her hands to her scalding cheeks.

"Get up," he seethed. "Now." The words were a gravelly whisper and barely tamped threat.

Her limbs itched to obey, but she braced herself instead, calling on every last ounce of bravery she could summon. She just prayed her body would re-member what it had to do, even if her mind was too scattered and panicked to focus.

The man bent to grab her, and she snaked her legs out to tangle with his. Then, in the way Dylan had taught her, she jerked the man off his feet.

And screamed, "Help!"

The thud of his collapse at her side nearly rattled her teeth. His weapon bounced free from his grip and skittered across the floor.

D.J.'s cries rose into the air, and she projected her voice to match his.

"Help!" she screamed, flipping onto her stomach and grabbing the fallen handgun. She flicked the safety off and pointed the gun at her intruder when he reached for her once more.

He turned his palms out, showing his surrender.

Behind her, the front door burst open and smacked against the wall. "Jen!" Knox bellowed.

She dared a glance in his direction, and witnessed his expression flow from fear to rage in the space of a heartbeat.

The sound of breaking glass drew her eyes back to the man in black once more. Now on his feet, he flung himself through the open window and onto her fire escape with a bewildering crash.

"Are you okay?" Knox asked, gripping her shoulders and searching her eyes.

"Yes."

He scanned her trembling body, before removing the gun from her frozen hands. "You're okay. I'm here," he assured, setting the weapon on her counter.

"Go," she said, her tears flowing anew. She thrust a hand toward the window. "Catch him."

Knox moved to the window in two steps. "He's almost to the bottom of the fire escape," he said, pulling his cell phone from one pocket and pressing it to his ear. "Lock the door behind me," he told her, blowing past her and into the building's hallway.

She slammed the door and flipped the locks, not needing to be told twice.

The sound of his fervent footfalls in the hallway outside brought her back to the moment at hand. She freed D.J. from his swing and hoisted him into her arms, then moved the gun to the end of the countertop, near the broken window.

Jen rocked and shushed her baby, kissing his soft curls and keeping watch, the broken window in view, and the gun in reach.

The next person through her window would be leaving with an injury.

Chapter Sixteen

Two hours later, Knox, Jen and D.J. were back at his place. He'd fielded a dozen calls from concerned family members while their statements had been taken by his fellow deputies at Jen's apartment. He could thank his brother's and uncle's police scanners for that. Cruz and Derek had decided they'd meet him at his house to go over the details in person. Which roughly translated to his big brother worrying unnecessarily and wanting to see for himself that Knox and the Jordans were unharmed.

Knox had reluctantly accepted, knowing the alternative was futile, and he'd warned them to keep it brief. The aftermath of Jen's shock had paled her skin and set her teeth to chatter. She needed rest, and that would be impossible while surrounded by people rehashing what she'd been through.

Thankfully, she seemed to slowly unwind at his place, apparently feeling safe and comfortable. Knox would've appreciated those facts more if his tension hadn't continually ratcheted since he'd first heard her scream. He'd allowed a gunman to break into her apartment while he was just down the hall, speaking to the building manager. He'd never imagined someone would climb the fire escape three floors and break a window, but he should have.

He should've thought of everything. Jen's and D.J.'s lives had counted on it.

He dragged a hand over his hair and forced himself to take long deep breaths, willfully slowing his temper and pulse. Jen's attacker was long gone. She and D.J. were safe. That was all that mattered.

He selected a pair of water bottles from his refrigerator and carried them to his living room, where Jen rested on the couch. Her teeth had stopped chattering from the excess and misplaced adrenaline and her cheeks had regained their color. Those details eased a measure of his tension, and he exhaled fully for the first time in hours.

"Thanks," she said, accepting the offered drink.

D.J. lay on his back before her, feet in the air and tugging off one sock with his busy little hands.

Knox watched as she sipped the water, slowly at first, then in deep thirsty pulls. "How are you feeling?" he asked. She'd barely allowed the medics to glance at her when they'd arrived at the apartment. She'd insisted on giving her statement immediately, and afterward she'd simply brushed the EMT off. Thankfully, the intruder had only shoved her and had never really gotten a chance to harm her. Knox wasn't sure he could've handled it if things had turned out differently.

According to her statement, Jen pegged the man at six feet tall, trim and with brown eyes. She also said he'd smelled of spearmint. It wasn't much of a description, but it was more than Knox could offer. He'd only seen the man for a moment before he dove onto the fire escape and ran away. If Knox was supposed to be Jen's personal protection, she needed to put a help-wanted ad in the paper, because he stunk.

"I'm going to be okay," she said, answering the question he'd nearly forgotten he'd asked. "All things considered, I'm still here with you and D.J., and I can't complain about that."

Knox tried and failed to return her small smile. His brows furrowed in frustration instead.

"How about you?" she asked. "You're awfully quiet."

He rolled his head to stretch the tense and aching muscles along his neck and shoulders. When that didn't work, he gripped and kneaded the knots with aggressive hands. "You shouldn't have had to defend yourself or face him on your own. I should've been there and I wasn't. And I hate it."

Jen sighed. "I figured that's what was bothering you."

"Can you blame me?" he asked, unable to hide the frustration in his tone. "I had one job."

She rolled her eyes. "Protecting me isn't your job. Getting to the bottom of this situation is, and that was what you were doing. We both believed I was safe inside my apartment, and you were letting Mrs. Hancock know to be on the lookout. You were spreading awareness and setting down a framework for finding this guy. That is your job. I'm smaller than you, but that doesn't make me helpless."

"That's not what I meant," Knox said. "This isn't a male/female thing. This is me feeling ashamed that I didn't do the one thing I promised to do. It might not be my exact job description, but I promised to protect you. And I never break promises. At least, not before now."

She cocked a brow and studied him.

"Hearing you scream," he said slowly, the sounds returning to him in a haunting echo. "Hearing D.J. cry. Knowing you were in trouble." He paused to wet his lips and check his composure. "That twisted something inside me so tightly I could barely breathe." He pressed a fist to his chest in illustration.

Knox had experienced all kinds of fear in his life, but none of it had compared to the possibility he'd be too late to save Jen and her son. He'd struggled to unlock and open her door, his thick frantic fingers devoid of agility. And he'd been sure all was lost on the other side.

The scene he'd walked in on had thrown Knox, almost as much as it had probably confused her assailant. Jen had a gun, and a man dressed in black was splayed on her floor.

It had taken longer than it should have for Knox's feeble mind to catch up.

She'd taken the man's gun.

And knocked him on his backside.

An unexpected chuckle broke through his pressed lips.

"What?" she asked, eyes narrowing.

"You attacked your attacker," he said, still awed. "And you won."

"I did," she said. "I can thank Dylan for that. He insisted I learn a few basic self-defense moves. He never wanted me to be a victim."

"You certainly aren't that," Knox said, crossing his arms and nodding. "I miss him, you know?" Knox hadn't seen Dylan in nearly two years before his death, but they'd stayed in touch online, and the distance hadn't seemed so big, nor had it diminished their friendship. He'd understood Dylan's need to keep fighting, and Dylan had understood Knox's desire to come home and protect folks in new ways.

"I miss him too," Jen said.

Knox watched as Jen stroked her baby's arms and cheeks. He admired the protective expression in her kind and loving eyes. "It took a lot of bravery to do what you did today," he said. "Knowing what to do is different than being able to do it when you're in danger. The guy had a gun. You still took him down." A torrent of pride swelled in his chest, and his smile widened to match hers.

"Well, I have a baby now," she said. "I had to do

something, and I couldn't afford to be afraid. Not if it meant D.J. might pay the price for my hesitation."

He nodded, admiration growing impossibly further in him.

"Now what are you thinking?" she asked, scooping D.J. into her arms. "Here. Sit. You're making me anxious."

Knox obeyed, taking the seat at her side. "I was thinking I like that you can handle yourself," he admitted. "I hate that I wasn't there for you, but I'm darn glad you didn't need me."

"Is that right?" she asked, a hint of disbelief in her voice. "I thought you hero-types tended to feel less manly when women saved themselves."

He laughed. The sound broke from his lips unexpectedly, and she laughed in return. "I'm just glad you're both okay. I don't care who did the saving."

Her expression softened, and her lips parted. "Yeah?"

"Yeah," he agreed. "And you won't catch me sneaking up on you anytime soon," he admitted, earning another broad smile.

"Smart man."

Their eyes met, and their smiles fell as the air around them seemed to charge.

D.J. set his cheek against his mother's collarbone and closed his eyes.

Jen snuggled her baby closer, and Knox felt the last of his resolve slip away. The little family before him had gained an unprecedented hold on his heart, and he wanted more than anything to let Jen know. He'd put off telling her for a dozen reasons, but being honest about his feelings, regardless of her response, seemed like the right thing to do. And if she didn't reciprocate, he was man enough, friend enough, to accept that without question or argument.

"What's wrong?" she asked.

"Nothing." He forced a smile and reminded himself he was a grown man, a former soldier, a lawman. Someone known for his bravery, and someone who shouldn't be afraid to tell the truth, even when the potential result posed a risk to his heart. "There's something I need to tell you," he said, willing the words from his lips.

"Okay." She shifted to face him, her expression somewhat…hopeful?

The doorbell sounded, changing his intended words to a growl.

Jen smiled. "Welcome to Winchester Country."

He groaned. "That makes it sound too fancy," he said, shoving onto his feet. "I changed my mind. I think we're more like a traveling circus."

The bell rang again as he strode into the foyer and opened the door to greet his guests.

Auntie Rosa patted his cheek as she and Uncle Hank bypassed him in search of his houseguests. They paused briefly to scan the area, then headed for Jen and D.J. By the time Knox made it back to the living room, his uncle had the baby in his arms and his auntie had pulled Jen into a hug. "We heard what happened and wanted to see you were okay with our own eyes," Auntie Rosa said, squeezing Jen tight.

"We're okay," Jen answered, stepping out of the embrace with a gentle smile. "We were lucky, and I'm glad we have somewhere safe to stay."

His auntie turned a bright smile on her husband. "All of my men are fully capable protectors and defenders, but Knox takes it to another level." She swung her attention to her nephew. "Always so serious. Always prepared to fight." Obvious pride flashed in her eyes. "It's nice to see him with something of his own to fight for."

Knox coughed, and tried not to give his auntie the pointed look she deserved. Jen might've been a champion swimmer, but Rosa was a world-class meddler. "Cruz and Derek are on their way," he said. "If you stick around a bit, you can get your hands on them too."

Auntie Rosa beamed. "I love when my family gathers. I can dole out hugs in bulk."

Jen laughed, then moved to Knox's side and slid her arm across his back. She rested her head against him, and his heart gave a heavy kick. "It's nice to have family near," she said softly, watching as his auntie turned to fuss over D.J. in Uncle Hank's arms. "I didn't realize how much I missed this."

"The fussing and intrusion?" he teased.

His auntie clucked her tongue, clearly eavesdropping.

Jen laughed. "Yes. All of it."

Across the room, his aunt and uncle fluttered and buzzed around her baby, attempting to comfort him or make him smile.

"He loves all this attention," she said. "Look at that big gummy smile."

Knox slid his arm across Jen's shoulders. It was true. D.J. was clearly in heaven.

The doorbell rang again, and Knox went to greet the newcomer.

Cruz waltzed passed. "Derek's a few minutes be-hind me. Hey, Jen."

She lifted one hand in a hip-high wave. "Hey."

Cruz kissed Auntie Rosa and shook their uncle's hand, then performed a lot of goofy baby talk for poor D.J.

Jen looked on in obvious delight. "It's really al-ways like this here?"

"Every day," Knox said, rubbing a palm against his cheek. "Not usually at my house, but in general, yes."

Cruz spun to face his brother and clapped his hands together sharply. "I didn't overhear anything useful at the clinic, but I noticed that only one of the doctors was there. Martz, I think. He showed up a couple hours after the staff. Shots and blood draws went on without him until he arrived. I called Derek when I heard you were attacked," he said, shifting his gaze to Jen. "He'll be here any minute to fill us in on his day."

As if on cue, the doorbell rang.

Cruz let Derek in and followed him back to the living room, where all eyes turned to his cousin.

"Well?" Cruz asked, falling onto the armchair and wedging one foot over the opposite knee. "I hope you learned more than me. My reconnaissance mission was an indisputable bust."

Derek greeted his mom and dad and the Jordans before turning a look of discouragement on his partner. "I didn't find anything useful at the receptionist's house, so I spent most of the day outside Dr. Abel's home on Willow Bend Lane. His car was in the garage when I got there and I took a peek around the perimeter. I sat in my truck and waited, but I never got eyes on him. No one came. No one left. I headed this way when I heard what happened at the apartment. I don't see how it could've been him if he was home the whole time, but I suppose he could have another car."

"Did you run a registration check with the DMV?" Cruz asked.

Derek shot him a bland look.

Knox took that as a yes, but Derek didn't elaborate.

Jen deflated onto the couch. The lightness in her eyes a moment earlier extinguished. "Do you think he stayed home today because he knew the deputies were interviewing at the clinic?"

"Maybe," Derek said. "I don't know what those doctors are up to, but it feels like something, and my instincts are never wrong." He shot Cruz another pointed look. "My contact at the DMV is pulling up Abel's vehicle registration."

Cruz nodded.

Jen looked to Knox, and he moved to her side. "I get the same feeling about the doctors," he said. "I don't like that Abel's name made that list. At least we can mark him off as the gunman. He couldn't have been at my place and at his. Any word yet on the other names?"

Cruz ran a hand through his hair. "Officially? I haven't heard anything, but they were all common first names."

"Clinic patients?" Jen guessed.

"Maybe," Cruz answered.

Knox gripped the back of the couch near Jen's shoulders, sorting through the new information. "Well, staying home won't keep the deputies from interviewing Abel, so that tactic will only work for a short while. They'll likely head over there when they finish downtown."

Jen swiveled on her seat, catching Knox in her suddenly wide gaze. "Can we go to his house?" she asked.

"Dr. Abel's?" he asked.

"Maybe he'll talk to me," she said. "Maybe he knows something that can help us. We assume he's a guilty party, but he could be afraid of someone else like Katie and Madison were. Maybe that's why his name made the list."

"That's a lot of maybes and unknowns," Knox

said. Which equated to a lot of risk. And he didn't want Jen anywhere near another source of danger. She'd been lucky to survive a gunman already today. "I think we should consider the offer to get out of town and move to the cabin. These guys can go knock on Abel's door and see if he's hiding from someone other than the sheriff's department."

Her jaw set, and his brother chuckled.

Derek rose and clapped a hand on Knox's shoulder. "I know I just met your girl, but that looks like a hard no to me."

Knox shook his cousin's hand away and glared at him, before catching his auntie's eye.

She'd apparently wrestled D.J. from Uncle Hank's grip and was busily smothering the baby with tickles and kisses. She raised an eyebrow. "Hank and I don't mind waiting here with this little sweetie if you all need to go somewhere for a bit," she offered, unhelpfully.

Knox groaned. He'd hoped that the risk involved in taking D.J. to a potential criminal's home would put an end to discussion on the outing.

Instead, all eyes turned to Jen.

Knox gritted his teeth while she deliberated. Maybe she wouldn't be comfortable leaving her son with someone she barely knew.

She pressed her lips together for a long moment. "Are you sure you don't mind?"

His auntie beamed. "Not at all. We'd stay here with this little man until he was eighteen if you wanted. I have my grandma supplies in the truck, stroller included, so we'll start with a long walk. I'll pack a picnic! Bananas and bottle for baby. Fresh fruit for Hank and me."

Delight crossed his uncle's features a moment before he blurred past Knox on his way out the door, presumably to fetch the stroller.

Cruz headed in the same direction. "Sounds like a road trip," he told Jen. "And you've got a three Winchester escort. Couldn't be any safer."

She rose and hurried after him.

Something told Knox this wouldn't be the last battle he lost against Jen and her accomplices, aka his too-accommodating family. And a smile spread across his face at the thought.

Chapter Seventeen

Knox followed his brother and cousin to Dr. Abel's home in West Liberty, one town beyond his jurisdiction as a deputy sheriff. He parked along the curb behind Cruz's big white Jeep and waited for the private detectives to climb out. He wasn't any happier about ringing the doorbell with Jen in tow now than he had been when they'd left his place, but she was adamant, and he was stuck.

She climbed out and rounded the hood to his side, nervously rubbing her palms against her thighs.

Knox offered her his hand and the most confident look he could manage. "Ready?"

She nodded.

The home was impressive and situated in the elite West Liberty Hills. The unique Frank Lloyd Wright–design style spoke volumes about the likely price tag, and the owner's desire to make a statement. Tall windows. Flat roofs. And an overall aesthetic that blended the home with the landscape. Private practice physicians made good money, but Knox wasn't wholly convinced the pay was enough to afford the sprawling property before them. He couldn't help wondering if MX-10 had somehow helped make the purchase possible. He made a mental note to find out how long the doctor had lived there.

Jen squeezed his fingers as they crossed the street.

Derek and Cruz had already disappeared, presumably checking the perimeter.

"Do you want to knock, or should I?" she asked.

Knox pressed the doorbell in response, eager to get this over with and hoping the guy didn't answer. His gut told him at least one of the doctors was trouble, and he needed to keep Jen as far away from trouble as possible. He couldn't bear to fail her again.

The bell chimed deep inside the home, but no sound or movement followed. He tried again, then turned to Jen, preparing to make his case for ending the mission.

A flicker of movement in his periphery swung Knox's attention to the attached garage. Derek stood in the driveway, his ear pressed to the closed door.

Jen frowned. "What's he doing?"

"I'm not sure," Knox said, tugging her away from the front door for a closer look at Derek. Knox lifted his chin in question when his cousin met his gaze.

"I smell exhaust," Derek said. "And I think I hear a car running."

Cruz appeared from around the corner, his expression dark as he lowered his face to the junction of garage door and driveway. "I smell it too. Call an ambulance," he said, shooting a look at Knox, before turning away.

Derek jogged to the nearby utility door and tried the knob. When that didn't work, he kicked the door in.

Jen squeaked as wood splintered, and the barrier banged open.

Cruz followed Derek inside.

"They shouldn't go in there," she said, staring wide-eyed as exhaust billowed through the busted door.

Jen might not have put the details together yet, but Knox had. Whoever was in Abel's garage wouldn't be any danger to them now.

Knox held her hand as he reported the facts to local dispatch.

The large door rolled slowly upward, and Cruz reappeared, T-shirt and arm pulled across his nose and mouth.

The sound of breaking glass was followed by the settling of a car engine, and Derek appeared seconds later. He doubled over at the waist, coughing and struggling for clean air.

"Abel?" Knox asked.

Cruz shook his head once. "He's gone. Probably been that way for a while now."

And Abel made death number two in as many days.

Not a good sign for Madison.

JEN THANKED HER lucky stars for the thousandth time that she hadn't brought D.J. along with her. If it hadn't been for Knox's aunt and uncle, she probably would've, and she couldn't imagine having him there now. Not with another tragedy nearby.

She'd been sure Dr. Abel would shed some light on what was happening. And that he wasn't the one trying to hurt her, so things were supposed to turn out okay. Having the Winchesters present had bolstered her confidence. All they'd needed, she'd thought, was to get Abel talking. That would never happen now.

Instead, another life had ended, and she was gutted by the senselessness of it all.

Her life had been beautifully ordinary only a few days before, but everything had changed. Madison's life had become entangled somehow with MX-10, and the drug might kill her without her ever taking a single pill.

Knox's shadow fell over Jen as he returned to her side. "My cousin Blaze is on his way," he said. "He's a West Liberty homicide detective. He was handling something at the prison, but he's leaving now. We've confirmed the man in the car is Dr. Abel. Cruz and Derek are going to wait out here. Why don't we take a look inside?"

She glanced over her shoulder at the picturesque home.

"We won't disturb anything," he said. "I'd just like you to see if you recognize anything as Madison's. Some sort of indication she's been here."

Her muscles tensed at the request. "You think she might've been here?"

"I think it's worth a shot," he said.

Jen followed Knox through the garage to the interior doorway, careful not to look in the direction of a small black Mercedes.

Knox held the door for Jen with his forearm. "Try not to touch anything."

She nodded, having no intention of leaving her mark upon the poor man's possessions. Her mind raced to the family and friends he'd left behind. Of all the people who'd get the awful call she had when Dylan died unexpectedly. Like Katie's family had yesterday.

The home's interior was as beautiful and well maintained as the exterior. Inviting, wide-open spaces were lined in tall narrow windows, most without blinds or curtains, allowing unobstructed views of the neatly manicured landscaping outside. The decor was minimal, but obviously high-end. Large furniture pieces had been neatly arranged in groupings and clusters throughout the rooms, creating the overall look of a magazine shoot instead of someplace a man had actually lived. Probably the work of an interior designer.

"Was Abel married?" Jen asked, realizing the home was far too large for one person, but far too tidy for a young family. Maybe the kids were grown? Or he was divorced? Maybe that was why so many spaces seemed more for show than function. A single person could likely only use a portion of the square footage with any regularity.

"I'm not seeing any signs of a roommate, spousal or otherwise," Knox said, leading the way through the main areas. "Shoes on the mat are all men's in the same size." He pointed to the entryway they'd passed through, then to a grand foyer on the left, where a pair of picture frames bookended a sculpture on an entryway table. One of the photos was of him and an elderly couple, possibly his parents. Another, of the doctor and a boat.

Knox ducked into an open bathroom in the hallway, then returned with a pair of tissues and offered one to Jen. "If you have to pick anything up."

She accepted with a nod.

The distant sound of sirens trickled into the sprawling home, a striking contrast to the bellowing silence around them.

Knox had shifted seamlessly from casual companion and protector to lawman. The change was visible in his stance and stride, the set of his jaw and the look in his eye. All evidence of the playful man she'd been with moments before was now wrapped tightly in a uniform and badge. Even if neither were physically with him.

He moved methodically through the home, a trained and sweeping gaze likely seeing more in a moment than she could if given an hour. Their first official stop was a home office with a library. Floor-to-ceiling windows graced the far wall, spilling natural light over hardwood floors, a massive mahogany desk and two walls of soaring bookcases. Under other circumstances, Jen would've been in love.

She inched toward the desk, feeling awkward and intrusive. Nothing of Madison's had been visible so far, and Jen wasn't sure what to look for otherwise.

She lifted a pen using her tissue as a barrier against her prints, then used the pen to open drawers and poke through the contents.

Knox concentrated on the bookshelves.

Nothing in the giant desk looked useful or seemed amiss, and she closed the final drawer with a sigh.

"Here," Knox said, urging her across the room with a tip of his head. "I've got something." He dialed his cell phone, then pressed it to one ear. "Hey," he said into the receiver. "There's MX-10 in the home office. About fifty pills." His eyes shut briefly. "No surprise there."

Jen followed his gaze when he opened his eyes.

He'd pulled a set of books away from the shelf and revealed a series of plastic baggies behind them, each with a small number of tablets like the ones found hidden under the sink in her apartment. "Looks like these were counted and ready for distribution," Knox said, sliding the phone back into his pocket. "Now, was this guy just a dealer? Or did he have a hand in the production too?"

Jen stepped away from the evidence, needing to put some distance between herself and the drug that seemed to be getting people killed. "How did you know they were there? There are thousands of books in here. A hundred shelves."

"These books weren't flush with the rest, but they're clearly part of this series," he said, pointing to the other tomes still standing on the shelf. "Plus, this shelf and set of books were clean, but the other shelves and books had a thin layer of dust on top. They'd obviously been recently moved, used or otherwise disturbed."

She considered taking a closer look, but decided to accept his word on the subject. Her mind had already jumped to a more important issue. "Abel's name was on the list at the carousel, and now he's dead," she said.

A look of understanding and compassion crossed Knox's face. He abandoned the stash of MX-10 in favor of meeting her near the door. "Why don't we check the rest of the house for signs of Madison?" he suggested. "Deputies will be here soon to handle the evidence. Meanwhile, we can check the property for places Madison could be held."

Jen's heart rate jerked into a sprint as she took his hand. Together, they backtracked to the garage, then started their exploration again. This time, opening every door, closet and cupboard.

"Madison!" she called, no longer able to contain the need to run, and Knox let her go.

He kept pace at her side, and together they cleared every floor, from attic to basement, before darting outside to check the grounds.

The street was full of first responders and emergency vehicles when they jogged into the yard. The late-afternoon sky was awash with carousels of red and blue. Uniformed men and women streamed in and out of the garage, across the tidy lawn and along the barricaded road at the end of the drive.

Jen's heart sank as Knox forced the door on the pool house open, revealing yet another unoccupied space. The last one on the grounds to check.

The feeling of loss hit like a brick, stealing her breath and stinging her eyes.

Once again, Madison was nowhere to be found.

KNOX CLOSED HIS front door for the last time at nearly midnight, hours after their return from Dr. Abel's home. The day had been long in every sense of the word, and his capacity to keep moving had dwindled almost completely. Thankfully, there was a fresh pot of coffee and plenty of questions to keep his tired mind engaged.

And there was Jen, who needed him to be strong.

She sat on the couch in her pajamas, looking cuddly and warm. She'd had a long shower after finally getting D.J. to sleep, and she'd emerged looking somewhat more relaxed. She should've been exhausted too, but her expression signaled fear more than fatigue.

Knox couldn't blame her for that. He was starting to seriously worry about her friend too. The bodies were adding up, and Madison had been missing for several days. More than he was comfortable with after seeing his share of missing women cases. The facts so far didn't set the stage for a happy ending.

Knox headed to the kitchen for coffee and hot tea, running mentally over all the details that had arrived in the last few hours.

Abel's death hadn't been labeled a homicide yet, but Knox's cousin Blaze suggested it was only a matter of time. The fact MX-10 was found in the car with the victim, and the initial coroner's report cited conditions pointing to drug use, Knox had to agree. The working theory was that Abel had taken some pills before getting into the car, likely with a little help. He'd passed out, then inhaled the exhaust fumes to the point of asphyxiation.

Deputy Wence was processing the gun used in the break-in at Jen's place and hoping for prints or ballistics to guide the investigation. The serial number had been scratched off, but if the gun had been used in any previous crimes, they would soon know.

The related conversations with Derek, Cruz and Blaze had been heavy and long, but Jen had listened carefully and asked excellent questions. Having her with them while they'd hashed things out had felt good. Natural. And his family members hadn't missed his pleasure in that fact. He'd seen it in their expressions as clearly as he'd felt it in his bones.

Knox carried a cup of hot tea and a mug of coffee to the living room, then set the tea on the coffee table for Jen. She'd switched from coffee after finishing her shower.

Knox drank deeply from his mug, then took the seat at her side. "How are you holding up?"

She gave a soft, humorless laugh. "Terribly. I'm shaken, terrified and getting angrier all the time. I hate that all this is happening."

"That's understandable," Knox said. "Stuff like this doesn't typically happen to law-abiding citizens. I'm sure it's confusing and infuriating." Knox set his mug aside. "You can talk to me about that if you want. Whatever you're feeling is valid. This is a lot to take in, and nearly impossible to process. I've investigated plenty of cases similar to this one on the surface, but something's not adding up this time."

"Agreed," she said, straightening with interest. "Aside from the fact Madison shouldn't be part of any of this, I keep wondering why Dr. Abel would get behind the wheel doped up. That doesn't make any sense. If he thought the sheriff's department was closing in on him for something, why not get rid of all those pills in his office? If a bad guy was threatening him, why not run? He had enough money to leave the country if he wanted."

"All good questions," Knox agreed.

"Do you think someone put the pills in his car and office to frame him?" she asked. "Why would he take a bunch of pills, then go sit in the car and inhale fumes? Seems like overkill to me. Don't both acts produce the same result?"

Knox nodded. "I suppose if he was an addict, he might've wanted one last high, or maybe he was just in a terrible headspace. He might've felt out of control, depressed or panicked, and he acted on it."

Jen reached for her tea, considering his words, but not arguing with them. "I guess. Speaking of bad headspace. Do you think Derek will be okay?"

"I think so," Knox said.

Derek had left shortly after Auntie Rosa and Uncle Hank. He'd blamed himself for not knowing Abel was in the car in the garage, when Derek had been right outside all day. A man had died only a few yards away, and Derek hadn't had any idea. He could've saved him, and that would haunt Derek for a long while to come. Knox knew because, logical or not, he'd feel the same way in Derek's place.

"Winchesters are made of some pretty tough stock," he added, appreciating Jen's concern for his cousin more than she could know. "He'll get through this. But I can see where he's coming from. We all do our best to be omniscient. We try to predict other people's motivations and reactions in order to maintain control, especially in difficult situations. It can be tough when we miss something. Especially something this big."

Jen sipped her tea, then set it aside. Her pensive expression faded slowly, and she turned to lean against his side.

His arm went around her on instinct, and it felt like the first true breath he'd taken in hours. He loved the way she felt in his arms, the way she fit so perfectly in his life and with his family. It was possible, he realized, that he was falling in love with Jen.

"Madison can't be dead," she whispered. "Because I can't lose someone else I love, and she's already been through too much. It just can't happen. She has to come home."

Knox pulled her closer. "No one is giving up on her," he promised. "Every new clue, each incident and uncovered fact, is leading us closer. It's just hard to see the progress when you're standing in the middle of the action. It might seem as if we're spinning in circles, but we are moving forward. I promise."

Jen twisted free of his arm, and tucked her legs beneath her, studying his features closely. "Madison's photo is all over the news, but no one knows where she is. No one has seen her since the night she was dragged away by a gunman in the park. Hope is getting a lot harder to find."

Knox reached for her hand, twining their fingers and giving an encouraging squeeze. "She's out there somewhere, and someone knows how to find her. All we have to do is keep looking. I'm here for that," he promised. "I will single-handedly turn over every stone in this county if I have to. Blaze and his brother, Lucas, will do the same in West Liberty. Plus, we've got Derek and Cruz. It's an all-star team," he said with a confident grin.

She smiled, and his heart ached to pull her against

him once more. How was she so darn perfect for him and how had he not told her yet?

"I'm glad you're with me," she said, expression softening. "I'd be completely lost if you hadn't decided to stay with me that first night and kept me with you every day since." She averted her eyes and bit into her lip, drawing his attention to her mouth. "I know you're just here as some kind of obligation to Dylan," she said, "but it means a lot to me. Probably more than it should."

"No," he interrupted. "That's not why."

She stilled and her brows rose. "Then you're here because it's your sworn duty to protect and serve."

"I'm on vacation," he whispered, bracing himself once more and willing the right words to come.

She smiled.

"It's true," he continued. "I heard you ask for me at the department, and I could never walk away from anyone asking for my help, but it became a lot more than that pretty quickly."

Her lips parted, and something akin to hope crossed her beautiful features.

"I knew I liked you that first night at your apartment," he said. "I also knew I shouldn't, because you were in trouble and needed a protector, not a boyfriend. But you're smart and kind, with a big admirable heart. I wasn't ready to leave when I easily could've gone. I used your potential need for protection as a reason to stay. And the longer we're together, the more I don't want to go."

Her blue eyes widened in pleasure, and a chill rippled over his skin. "What if I want you to stay?" she asked, sounding a little breathless. "Even when this is over?"

"Then I'll stay," he answered simply. "I've grown unreasonably attached to you, and your son."

Her lips twitched, fighting a small smile.

Knox's heart began to pound.

"Is that what you wanted to tell me earlier, before you were interrupted?"

"Yes. And I know the timing is terrible. You're in the middle of something awful. Emotions are high. The future is uncertain. The last thing I want to do is make you uncomfortable with my proclamations."

Jen's gaze dropped to his mouth, silencing him instantly. "Knox," she said, "the only thing making me uncomfortable right now is the fact you still haven't kissed me."

Chapter Eighteen

Knox felt his brow furrow, even as a wide smile spread over his face, and he lowered his mouth to hers. The confusion about how he could be fortunate enough to gain her desire vanished when their lips met, and all he could think about was the taste of her. Heat flooded over him until what he'd planned to be a respectable and chaste exchange quickly deepened.

Jen's arms wound around his neck, and she rose onto her knees, bringing them closer.

He inhaled her sweet scent and devoured her delicious moans.

The warmth and weight of her body against his sent his heart and mind into the atmosphere. And he knew it was a turning point from which he would never fully recover.

His hands spanned the width of her back, and he glided his palms along her spine, memorizing and cataloguing every dip and curve. His fingers trailed a path over her ribs until his thumbs found the underside of her breasts, warm and enticing beneath the thin cotton shirt.

She sucked an audible breath in response.

Knox stilled. He pulled back an inch and looked into her wide blue eyes. "Are you okay?" he asked. "Is it too much? Too fast?"

Jen shook her head, a dazed but pleased expression on her beautiful face. "I'm in absolute heaven."

He smiled at her description of the moment.

"There had only been room for one man in my life since the moment I realized I was pregnant," she said. "Until now."

A familiar swell of pride bloomed in his chest. The knowledge she wanted him in her life was mind-boggling. A complete aphrodisiac and one heck of an ego boost.

He dropped a line of grateful kisses along the column of her throat, alternating gentle nips with comforting swipes of his tongue. He cradled her head in his hand when she arched, exposing more of her flushed skin.

Her narrow fingers found the hem of his shirt and dragged it upward, forcing him to release her long enough to strip the material away.

His muscles flexed and contracted beneath her teasing fingers, and he longed to return the favor.

She broke the kiss again too soon. Then, apparently reading his thoughts, she removed her shirt with one sharp lift of her arms.

To his immense shock and extreme pleasure, she'd forgone a bra.

A guttural moan ripped through him as his hands returned to her sides. He gripped her tightly and lifted her over him until her thighs bracketed his. Then he lowered his mouth to her bare skin and lavished her with kisses.

Jen's fingers knotted in his hair, and a series of sexy encouragements fell from her lips. "I'm not going to break," she said, arching into his touch. "I want you. And I don't want you to hold back."

Knox raised his eyes to meet hers once more. Eager to please them both, but hesitant to ruin the moment by pressing his luck. "I don't want to rush you, and I'm in no hurry."

Jen pulled his mouth back to hers and lowered fully onto his lap.

His obvious, undeniable arousal was a testament to how much he wanted her too.

Then she rocked her hips, and Knox's inner gentleman left the building.

JEN DRAGGED HER eyes open later, temporarily confused by the scene around her. Silver rays of moonlight streamed through Knox's bedroom curtains and over her thoroughly sated body. The scent of him on her pillow, and on her skin, drew a pile of vivid, beautiful memories into her mind.

She'd asked him not to hold back, and he'd responded by raising the bar on intimacy for eternity. Definitely the smartest request she'd ever made.

A small laugh broke on her tongue, and she rolled to see if she'd woken him.

The sheets beside her were mussed, but cool and empty.

The home was quiet, save for the sounds of soft male singing in the kitchen.

She stretched onto her feet and tugged one of Knox's T-shirts over her head, then padded quietly toward the tune, shamelessly proud. She'd made Knox Winchester sing.

The refrigerator door was open as she entered the kitchen, lending a cone of soft white light to the space. Knox straightened and peered at her over the divide. A low cuss ripped from his mouth. "Are you wearing my shirt?"

Jen grinned. "I guess I should've asked. I can take it off, if you'd like."

"Get over here." Knox shut the fridge and pulled her to him. He kissed her lips, then set her on his countertop and offered her the bottle of cold water in his hand.

"Couldn't rest?" she asked, sipping gently, and hoping he hadn't gotten out of bed because he didn't want to sleep with her.

Uncertainty doused her warm thoughts like ice water, and she crossed her arms over her chest in embarrassment. In some ways, waking up together was as intimate as anything they'd done before falling asleep. Maybe she'd gotten carried away. Maybe she was the one who'd moved too fast.

Maybe Knox was one of those men who didn't do relationships.

"Why are you single?" she asked, ripping the proverbial bandage off her heart before she became more injured than necessary.

Knox's easy smile halted her emotional spiral. "It's been a long time since I found someone who interested me more than my work."

She contemplated the deeper meaning, hoping but unsure. "I see." He was on vacation now, and it was probably stupid of her, but she was determined to soak up every available ounce of him until he went back to work. Better to have a few days of bliss in his arms than to go their separate ways later, and wonder what it would've felt like to be the one he kissed good-night.

She set a palm against his bare chest and worked up a small smile. "Does that mean I have your attention now?"

Knox's eyes went dark as he stalked closer, removing the bottle from her hand and nudging her knees apart with his hips. He gripped her thighs and brushed his lips against hers. "Jen," he said with reverence. His palms slid beneath the hem of her shirt, and he pulled it over her head, leaving them skin to skin once more. "You have all of my attention, for as long as you want it."

She released a long happy breath, hoping there

was a scenario where that would be true long-term. His sharp green eyes appraised her when she hesitated, then she pushed the doubts aside and kissed him deeply.

His responding growl rumbled beneath her roaming hands.

"I really like your attention," she said between kisses, feeling a smile spread his lips.

"It's all yours," he confirmed, leaning her back on the counter with an appreciative, hooded stare.

She arched sharply in response to his talented, confident touch.

"Keep that up," he said, "and I'll call in tomorrow and resign."

She clutched his wrist as desperation rose in her once more. "Keep that up," she countered, "and I will gladly let you resign."

Then she fell apart before he could argue.

Chapter Nineteen

The bed shifted beneath Jen, rousing her once more. A phone buzzed softly nearby.

It only took a moment for her to realize Knox was still with her. He'd brought her back to bed, and he'd stayed through the night. Her heart leaped as she turned in search of his handsome face.

But he'd already rolled away, sitting on the bed's edge, the phone pressed to his cheek.

"Yeah?" he answered roughly, the husky growl of sleep in his voice.

Jen held her breath, fighting the pang of uncertainty. She'd never been in a real relationship until Dylan, and being with him had been nothing like being with Knox. Life with Dylan had been a series of flirtations and teases, dates and romps. Their time had been easy, carefree and youthful. She'd only truly begun to let her whole guard down a short while before his death, and he'd never seen her at her worst. Knox had met her at her worst and lived with her in a state of emotional and physical dishevelment all week. The stakes were impossibly high, and everything around them felt intense and heavy.

"No," he said quietly to whoever had called. "I'm up. Just trying not to wake Jen or the baby." He twisted at the waist for a look in her direction. An expression of surprise was replaced by a smile when their eyes met.

She breathed again, attempting to look at ease, and likely failing miserably.

Knox rose, then leaned across the bed to press a kiss against her forehead. "All right," he said into the phone's receiver. "We'll be here." He disconnected the call and tossed the phone onto the bed. "It's breakfast time with the Winchesters," he said. "Cruz, Derek and Blaze are on their way over. Sounds like they're bringing food. All we need to prepare is coffee."

He pulled a shirt over his head, then froze when their eyes met once more. "What's wrong?" He scanned her face and tense form beneath his sheets. "Is it us?" he asked, motioning vaguely between them, a frown marring his brow.

"Maybe," she admitted, wanting to be truthful, but hating the catch in her voice. "I don't regret last night, but this is awkward, right?"

Knox returned to the bed. "How?"

She pressed her lips, then blew out a sigh. "You were Dylan's best friend. I was his fiancée, and your family knows that. What will they think?" She averted her gaze. "Not that there's any reason for them to know."

Knox stretched out on the bed beside her, propping his head on one hand. "We both loved Dylan. That connection will always be between us, and it's unusual, but it's not wrong."

She huffed a small breath, eyes stinging suddenly with unexpected tears.

"You told me yourself that you aren't the same woman he knew," Knox said, earning the return of her gaze. "You've changed. And even if you hadn't, I know he'd want you to be happy. I want you to be happy. And, Jen, I would never do anything to intentionally make you cry." He reached for her cheek and swiped away a falling tear.

She covered his hand with hers and held it to her cheek. "Thanks."

Knox nodded, searching her face for something more. "After my mama died, there were times when going on without her was even harder than losing her, if that makes any sense."

"Yeah," Jen said, swallowing past the lump in her tightening throat. "It does."

"I think we owe it to the ones we've lost to keep on living," Knox said. "To do good in this world, to find joy and make them proud." He swept sleep-wrecked hair from her cheek and smiled. "I'm not here to push or rush you, and I understand if you're seeing things differently by light of day. It won't weaken my dedication to protecting you and Dylan Jr."

Jen pressed a kiss to his palm, infusing the act with her gratitude. "What about your family?" she asked. They would surely need to explain themselves to a family as involved in one another's lives as his. Wouldn't they?

"We'll tell them as much as you want to tell them, when you're ready to tell them, but I've got to be honest with you. They're all detectives of their own accord, and a bunch of shameless gossips where family is concerned. I'm sure they already know."

A bolt of alarm burst through her at the thought. They knew? "About this?" she squeaked, and clutched the sheets more tightly to her chest.

Knox laughed. "About my intentions."

"Your intentions?" she repeated, loosening her white-knuckled grip on the material. A self-deprecating smile twisted her lips. "With a woman managing a missing friend and a baby?" She shook her head. "There's no pressure here. I know I come with baggage."

Knox's expression turned cold. His brows furrowed and his lips pulled down at the corners. He lifted her chin with his fingertips and trapped her in his piercing green gaze. "You aren't pressure, Jen. You're a prize. You got that?" He dropped a kiss on her forehead, cheeks and nose, repeating the pattern until her smile returned.

"Okay," she agreed.

"Good." He rolled away and rose fluidly from the

bed, then cast her a wicked grin. "Now hurry up and get dressed before my family finds you in here naked."

KNOX REFILLED COFFEE mugs while keeping tabs on the conversation with his brother and cousins, as well as one eye on Jen and D.J. The Winchesters were spitballing, brainstorming and attempting to piece together what they knew about the MX-10 epidemic and its apparent connection to Madison, Katie and Abel. As well as the names on the list at the carousel. Jen was playing on the living room floor with her son, while thumbing through the stack of notebooks she'd taken from her roommate's desk.

Blaze tapped a finger against the open folder before them. Autopsy results, complete with photos, lay on the table beside the emptying plates of fruits, cheeses and muffins his wife, Maisy, had sent along. "The coroner found no evidence of emissions in Abel's lungs," Blaze said. "He was definitely dead when he got into the car."

"No surprise there," Derek said, exchanging a look with Cruz. "The question now is how'd a dead man get into a car and start the engine?"

Knox set the pot back on the coffee maker and resumed his seat at the table. "So, we've got two murders. Katie's and Abel's."

"Yeah." Blaze scrubbed a hand over his unshaven face and stretched back in his seat. "The list at the park had both Madison's and Abel's names on it. She was taken. He was killed. Katie's name wasn't on the list, but she's also dead. So where does that get us?"

Cruz frowned. "Incomplete list?"

"All three victims worked at the clinic," Derek said. "So there's an undeniable connection to that location."

Knox nodded. "Agreed. Could the other names be additional staff?"

"Nope," Cruz answered. "I got a list of employees from the sheriff's department after they finished with their questioning. Derek and I are assisting officially now, on reconnaissance and research. I'll be running background checks on the other employees, but my money's on that other doctor, Martz."

"Any chance we know if the names are patient names?" Knox asked, knowing it was a long shot, considering the regulations surrounding privacy and health care.

Blaze shook his head. "It'll take a warrant and a miracle to get access to patient names."

Derek tipped his chin at Cruz. "Maybe you can use your pretty face and some sweet talk to grease a few lips at the office. The clinic employees know their coworkers are dying. Find a staffer who'll tell you if there are patients with the same names as those on the list. You don't have to ask for last names. No sensitive information. Just do they or don't they have at least one patient by each name."

Cruz sucked his teeth, contemplating. He'd made sport of using his charm and personality to get whatever he wanted until a short while ago, when he'd met Gina. He'd grown a bit of a conscience since then that Knox normally appreciated. At the moment, his opinion was on the fence.

"I can ask," Cruz said. "No promises. And whatever I learn won't hold much weight."

"Agreed," Knox said. "The names were fairly common. It's reasonable to assume we'd find matches in any group larger than a couple dozen. The clinic probably sees hundreds of folks every year."

Blaze nodded. "We can run on the assumption they were clients, or at least affiliated with the clinic, for now. That gets us to the likelihood that the drugs are linked to the facility as well. It'll be easier to get a warrant to search the premises than the patient files. So, I'll work on that." He swiped his phone to life and tapped the screen, presumably setting the ball in motion for a warrant.

Knox cast another look into the living room and caught Jen looking back. She smiled, and it reached his lips as well. When he returned his attention to the table, the other men stared in open curiosity. Cruz smirked, but nodded slightly with smug approval.

As predicted, his family saw everything.

Blaze set his phone aside and rolled his shoulders. "In a twisted way, Abel's death might be good news for Madison. A second associated murder is pushing her missing person case to the top of the local law enforcement priority list."

Jen's attention snapped to Blaze. "Have you learned anything new?"

Blaze nodded. "I had a feeling this case was headed my way, so I contacted the guys over at the sheriff's department, and they brought me up to speed. So far, I learned the boot prints near the carousel were a size larger than any of the boots found in Abel's house, and the treads didn't match. So he wasn't the one who took her, and wasn't likely the gunman you saw in the park."

"Or the one in my apartment," she said, putting the facts together.

"Not according to time of death," he agreed.

Jen rose onto her knees, and the memory of seeing her do the same thing last night flashed into Knox's mind. In the next moment, she'd kissed him like she'd longed for it. And things had only gotten better from there.

Cruz leaned in close and positioned his mouth near Knox's ear. "You need a little privacy for those thoughts?" he whispered. "Maybe a napkin to wipe up the drool?"

Knox snapped back to reality, then locked his jaw when both Cruz and Derek laughed.

Thankfully, neither Blaze nor Jen seemed to have noticed. They hadn't missed a beat in their exchange.

"You think Abel got the pills through the clinic somehow?" she asked. "Maybe his dealer is the one who took Madison. She might've found out what was going on and told Katie." Her eyes flashed with fear.

"Tell me there's a chance whoever killed Abel and Katie hasn't already…" She trailed off, unable to finish the awful thought.

That the killer behind two known murders might have already committed a third.

Blaze offered a patient but confident look. "We'll find her."

Jen lowered back to the floor with a nod. She scooped her baby into her arms and buried her face in his soft curls. Then returned to the pages of Madison's notebooks once more.

Knox longed to go to her, but sensed she needed a little space and time. Especially in the presence of his family. So he forced his attention back to the discussion at hand.

Where was the MX-10 coming from? Who had killed the doctor and receptionist? And where was Madison?

The conversation was slow and heavy, like wading through quicksand, examining known evidence for an aspect or detail they'd somehow overlooked. The need for new information was increasingly painful. And an hour later, nothing in the case file had moved them forward in their search for answers.

"Knox?" Jen said, drawing his eyes to her once more.

Her attention was fixed on a page thick with writing, and her lips were parted, as if she'd paused midthought.

"What do you have?" he asked.

She raised a bewildered expression to the men at the table. "I think I found the original list from the carousel." She turned the notebook around in evidence. "Madison wasn't finished writing at the park. The last name on this list is Dr. Martz."

Chapter Twenty

Jen paced the living room with D.J. fighting sleep against her chest. She rocked and bounced to soothe his whimpers and complaints as much as to burn her restless energy. Knox's home had been a tense flurry of activity after she'd shown the Winchesters Madison's notebooks. The detective and PIs were gone now, but her pulse still raced from the crash of voices and activity that had ensued.

The men had swarmed her, examining the notebook in her hand as well as all the others Jen had brought from Madison's room. They'd photographed multiple pages, then torn them from their flimsy spiral binding.

Knox had scanned and printed copies of every page of interest, then secured the sheets inside clear plastic sheaths for their protection. His brother and cousins had made phone calls, spoken in acronyms and stormed around, setting plans based on the new information, before blowing out the door one by one. Each on his own mission.

The general commotion and deep rumbling of authoritative male voices had worked D.J. into a fit, and Jen had spent her time distracting and calming him. She'd missed most of what had been said, and eventually had to leave the room to help her baby find his calm. Now, the home was quiet. Knox had walked his brother out and D.J. was nearly asleep, though determinedly resisting.

She only wished she could sleep as well. Her insides were tight with worry and her mind spinning with unanswered questions, old and new. Wouldn't it be nice to be rocked to sleep and wake up at a different place on her timeline. Even a few hours from now, when her nerves had calmed and her son was rested. It would be even better to wake when Madison was home safely and the worrying was done. Jen was tired in her bones and in her soul. She'd been that way for more than a year, if she were being honest, and the only time she'd felt any true respite had been in Knox's arms.

She wasn't sure if that made her weak or something worse, but it had been true nonetheless. She'd underestimated the value in feeling safe, seen and cared for when her life had been filled with feelings like those. She wouldn't be so quick to take anything for granted in the future.

The front door opened, and Jen started, frozen temporarily in place.

Knox lifted a hand in apology. "Sorry." He secured the locks and rested his hands on his hips, thoughts racing behind troubled green eyes. "Blaze is on his way to talk with Dr. Martz at the clinic," he said. "Derek's going to try the doctor at his home. Hopefully, one of them catches him. They'll be in touch to coordinate the interview."

"And Cruz?" Jen asked, pressing a kiss to D.J.'s forehead when his soft snore reached her ears.

"Cruz is also on his way to the clinic, but he plans to schmooze an admin out of as many details and insights as possible." Knox grinned and shook his head, as if there was more to that story, but he didn't go on.

Instead, he headed for the kitchen table, still covered in printed photos of the notebook pages. The originals had gone with Blaze.

"If we're right, and Martz is involved with MX-10 in any capacity, it'll ruin him professionally," Knox said. "If he's the one making and distributing the pills, he's looking at more than the loss of respectability and his medical license. He'll be put in jail and held accountable for the lives he's ruined, not to mention the ones he's taken."

Jen returned to her seat across from his. "You think Dr. Martz is the killer."

The tension in his limbs and jaw confirmed as much, but Jen needed to hear him say it. There wasn't any room left in her cluttered, terrified mind for guesswork or assumptions.

Knox nodded. "Abel's and Katie's deaths, Madison's abduction and your recent attack."

"Okay," she said, steeling her nerve and pushing

past the dream of sleeping until the worst had passed. Fighters didn't hide, and she'd never been anything else. "What can we do? Don't say sit tight and be patient," she said. "There has to be some way we can help, even from here."

Knox flexed his jaw several times before he met her eye again. "How are you at online research?"

She smiled. "I can find people on social media as needed, and if I know the city where they live, I can usually find a little more."

Interest lit his gaze. "Such as?"

"Their home address, using the local auditor's site, assuming they bought their home. With that information, I can find images of their home with Google Maps, and sometimes the interior as well, if the sales pages haven't been removed from the realtor sites."

Knox leaned forward on the table. "Marital status?"

"Sure. If it's not noted on their Facebook profile, I can check public records. Marriage license applications and divorce filings are all public record," she said.

"Do I want to know why you know how to find all that?" he asked.

"Women are frequently endangered, injured or killed at the hands of a date or spouse," she said. "We're taught that practically before we're out of diapers, so I've long made it a practice to know who my friends and I are trusting with our lives before heading out on dates or getting serious with anyone. Some guys are just married liars too, so there's that."

Knox performed a slow blink. "I forgot who I was dealing with for a minute," he said. "My apologies." He tried and failed to suppress a smile, and Jen sat taller in response. "Why don't you take another look at the list of names from the carousel wall and notebook?" he asked, selecting the photo of the page in question from the table. He set the paper in front of Jen. "See if you can find their social-media profiles and if there's a common thread Blaze or the deputies can pull. Now that we have last names to work with, maybe something useful will turn up. I'll review the staff's background checks," he said. "Looking for commonalities."

He rose and made a trip to his desk, then returned with a pair of laptops. He placed one covered in travel and sports stickers in front of her, then set a more serious-looking black computer before himself.

Jen excused herself to settle D.J. in his crib, then returned quickly to the table, eager to get started. She eased the lid open and powered the device on, prepared to do her best to oblige and impress. A moment later, an image of Knox and Cruz with a woman who, based on the matching thousand-watt smile and pale green eyes, could only be their mother appeared. The men were younger, somewhere in their teens with floppy unkempt hair, sun-kissed cheeks and imperfect complexions. Knox had braces. Cruz was in a baseball jersey. The woman glowed with all the unapologetic joy of a mom thoroughly in love with her two perfect sons.

"She was healthy there," he said, drawing Jen's attention to him. "That was the last one of Cruz's ball games we attended together before her diagnosis. She was planning a family vacation, because he was leaving soon. Either to a career in professional baseball or to college on a full athletic scholarship, anywhere he wanted to play."

Jen glanced at the photo again, applying ages to the men. Cruz was a high school senior there, which made Knox barely old enough to drive. Why this was their last game together was still unclear. "Was it the last game of the season, or did you lose her before he graduated?" Jen asked.

"Neither." He smiled, a distant, unfocused look in his eyes, seeing something in his past she couldn't begin to guess. "He quit."

"Quit baseball?" Jen guessed, assuming he hadn't meant high school, but quitting a sport he was apparently so good at seemed equally unbelievable.

Knox nodded. "Yeah. She wasn't given much time, right from the start, so he and I made it our jobs to spend every minute we could with her. We attended every treatment. Missed a lot of school, but the teachers were understanding. They gave us extra time on assignments and made lots of provisions. Small-town benefits, I guess. Everyone knew and loved Mama." He returned his gaze to Jen, steadying himself, before going on.

Jen waited patiently, eager for the details but unwilling to rush him about anything so important.

"We held her hair back when the chemo made her sick. Shaved her head for her when she was ready. Cared for her when she was weak. And we were both there when she left us," he said. "Cruz sensed it before I could. Maybe because I was younger. Maybe he's just always been more in tune with people. He told her we'd be okay. That we had Auntie Rosa and Uncle Hank to keep us in line, and that she was the perfect mother. So, the work for Rosa and Hank wouldn't be hard. Then he said we'd see her again one day." Knox cleared his throat. "He handled everything like a man, comforted me like a dad, when he was just a kid himself. He joined the military instead of playing ball and sent money home frequently to help with her medical bills. I stayed with our aunt and uncle until I graduated. Then I did the same. Cruz seems like he's carefree, but he's the most conscientious, grounded and caring person I know. That's saying a lot because I know some pretty great people."

Jen's eyes misted, and she reached for Knox's hand. How had the women in his life before her ever let him get away? How could anyone know him and not love him?

She squeezed his palm, not even a little startled by the path her thoughts had taken. Her heart was already his. "Thank you for sharing that with me," she said. "I'm glad to get to know you better. And the fact you made time to let me, even in the midst of this—" she motioned to the laptops and case evidence peppering the table "—means more to me than you know."

His cheek lifted with a lazy half smile. "I want you to know me. And I want to know you." He lifted their joined hands and pressed a kiss to her knuckles before letting go and setting his fingers on his laptop keyboard.

She flashed him a bright smile, then turned back to the machine before her.

They worked in companionable silence for a long while before taking a much-needed break.

Knox pushed away from the table and stretched to his feet. "I would never survive a desk job," he said, rolling his shoulders and twisting gently at the waist. "Have we eaten since breakfast?"

"You had an apple," Jen said, suddenly famished at the thought of food and wishing she'd had an apple too. "Should we make something?" she asked. "We can discuss our findings over whatever mealtime this is?" She turned on her seat in search of a clock.

"I've got this," he said, heading for the fridge. "Did you have any luck connecting the people on the list outside the clinic?"

"None," she said. "Other than the fact they all live in the same county, which I could've guessed, given the fact they all chose a doctor here. That's where the commonalities seemed to end. There's a high school athlete, a local college honor student, a couple of professional dancers, a judge, an ophthalmologist and a few women who have home-based businesses." She arched in her seat, stretching her aching neck and shoulders.

Knox crossed his arms and rested his backside against the countertop. "All those professions sound high-stress," he said. "That might be the link between them. A dope-peddling doctor might've suggested he could help them relax." He pursed his lips a beat, as if considering his own suggestion. "I'll mention it to Blaze and the deputies."

She nodded. "What did you learn about the clinic employees?"

"They had a few things in common," he said. "None have criminal records, but they're all in precarious financial situations. Recently divorced, working two jobs, living alone in the area with loose or no known family ties. And aside from a phlebotomist with a certification, no one on staff has any specific qualifications. No college degrees. No extensive experience or training."

"Is that legal?" Jen asked, recalling all the people she'd seen in scrubs at the clinic. "No nurses?"

"No nurses, and it's legal," he said. "Anyone can check a patient in, weigh them, take vitals and complete charts. The phlebotomist draws blood and gives shots. Other than that, the doctors seem to handle things. It's possible Martz sought employees he felt would be loyal to him for the opportunity. I'm guessing a more than fair wage helps seal lips as well."

Jen frowned. "I'd say it's awful and shameless to

manipulate people in need, but I suppose he's done much worse. And I can see how Madison fit the bill. She's new to the area, has no family nearby and struggles with the loss of her husband."

"By design, it should've been easy for any of the employees to look the other way if they saw something questionable going on," Knox said.

"Easy for anyone except Madison."

He nodded. "I'm guessing that's exactly how all this began. She might've had a suspicion that needed to be confirmed before going to the police. I can see why she didn't clue you in on what she was up to."

Jen's lips curled into a slight smile. "She always does the right thing. I should've known her painstaking goodness had something to do with the trouble she's in. I hate that I ever doubted her," Jen said. She hadn't gone all-in thinking Madison had slipped up, but she had wondered, initially, if Madison had made a wrong decision somewhere along the line. Trusted a wrong person, or otherwise inadvertently started the ball rolling downhill.

Of course her friend had seen something dangerous happening and wanted to stop it.

Knox's phone rang as he removed a loaf of bread from the pantry. "Yeah?" he answered, gaze drifting to Jen as he listened to the caller. "Sounds good. We'll meet you there. We were just about to eat anyway."

Jen's stomach tightened and her muscles tensed. His expression was unreadable. Was he attempting to cover bad news?

He pocketed the phone, then put the bread away. "Wence says she's headed to Coffee Cat to interview employees in about an hour. She thought we might want to sit in on some of the discussions. How do you feel about getting a bite to eat there while we wait for her to arrive and get started?"

Jen rose with a smile. "Give me ten minutes to change D.J. and pack his bag."

"I've got the bag," Knox said. "You do you. I'll handle this. Bottles. Diapers. Monkey rattle and those weird puffed cereal bits. Yeah?"

Jen paused, grateful and warmed once more by Knox's easy willingness to help, even when the task was small and she hadn't asked. "Thanks."

He winked, and her heart gave a heavy kick.

She would be lost and miserable if he left when Madison returned, so she hoped like crazy that he might want to stay.

Chapter Twenty-One

Traffic was thick and slow around Coffee Cat. The sidewalks teemed with people, and Jen felt the familiar pangs of fear return.

"What's going on?" she asked. "Is it always so congested at this hour?" She checked the time on Knox's dashboard clock and groaned. No wonder she was hungry. It was twelve thirty.

Lunchtime.

"Yeah," Knox answered belatedly. "There are a lot of popular restaurants on this block."

"Great." She swung her gaze in search of a parking spot but came up empty.

Knox circled the block, then doubled back in the opposite direction on a second pass.

The clinic parking lot was on her right.

"You see that?" he asked, pointing through the windshield. "All those men and women in black ball caps and windbreakers are deputies."

Jen followed his gaze, not seeing the hats or jackets at first, then becoming hyperaware. There were three men in black windbreakers just outside the truck, and another two near the corner. They blended with the moving crowd, when she wasn't looking for them, but now that she was, it was easy to see they weren't going anywhere. They were meandering. Maybe searching for something.

Or someone.

Knox drummed his thumbs against the steering wheel. "Something's going on."

Jen trailed one of the deputies with her gaze as he threaded his way through the pedestrians, head turning slowly side to side.

Knox cursed. "Hold on."

The truck darted forward a few feet when the light turned green, then rocked to a stop on a wide patch of concrete at the corner of a large full parking lot. He released his safety belt, then stretched an arm behind the seat and came up with a small domed emergency light. "There." He set it on the dashboard and turned it until the Jefferson County Sheriff's Department sticker was visible through the windshield. "I might still get a ticket, but I can't keep circling the block. I'll go insane. Plus, I want to know what's going on."

Jen frowned. "I'd be more worried about being towed than getting a ticket. Will that little thing really help?"

He turned a mock-offended look her way, one hand still resting on the light. "This is an official mini-beacon," he said. "Not a little thing."

"Oh." She fought a smile. "I see. I'm very sorry."

He nodded, then opened his door.

"It's just that my cousin had one of those in her room for karaoke dance parties when we were eleven," Jen said as genuinely as she could manage.

Knox pointed a warning finger at her, then unfastened D.J.'s harness and lifted him from the car seat. "Your mama thinks she's funny," he told her baby. "Good thing she's so cute."

Jen snickered as she met him at the grill of the truck, then accepted her perfect baby boy from Knox's careful hands. "I was only joking," she said. "I think your little flasher is adorable."

Knox snorted. "Don't let my family hear you say that."

She produced a wicked smile, then slid D.J. into the sling and headed for the coffee shop.

Knox easily kept pace. He slid his hand around hers and pulled her to his side. "Once we get in line, I'll text Wence and see what she can tell me about all the deputies down here. We'll wait to see if the interviews are still on schedule, or if they're being postponed, and if so, why?"

"Any guesses about what's happening?" Jen asked, fear scraping at her bravado once more. What if someone else was hurt, or worse? And what if that person was Madison?

Knox opened the coffee shop door for her, then took the place in line at her side. "Other than they seem to be looking for something or someone, no," he said. "The absence of uniforms makes me think they're trying to be discreet."

Jen turned to the menu board, trying not to think of what the new information could mean for Madison. Her stomach growled at the sight of all the delicious options.

Knox set a palm against her back as they inched forward. "Chicken bacon ranch panini. I think those might be my new four favorite words."

"I'll try that too," Jen said, thankful the long line was moving quickly.

Knox pulled his phone from his pocket and began to dance his thumbs across the small screen.

Jen scanned the busy café and hummed to D.J. while she waited for news from Deputy Wence.

"Next," the woman at the counter called, motioning Jen ahead.

"Two chicken bacon ranch paninis and two bottles of water," she said, unwilling to interrupt Knox for a drink order.

She paid the bill, then moved to the end of the counter.

Knox ghosted along at her side, eyes fixed on his screen.

"Okay," he said a moment later, pocketing the phone and stepping into her personal space. "Wence says someone called in a tip about Madison. They claim they saw her on the news, and think she's being held in the building near the clinic."

"Which building?" Jen said, her attention jerking to the window overlooking the street. "Is she okay?"

He shook his head. "We don't know. A team is clearing each building floor by floor. The deputies outside are watching for suspicious activity. In case whoever took her tries to move her."

"Chicken bacon ranch paninis," a man behind the counter called. "Two waters."

"Here." Jen raised her hand and Knox accepted the tray.

Together, they moved to the only open table, a two-seater near the far wall.

Knox angled his chair for a view of the window, and Jen followed suit.

"Where's the team now?" Jen asked, pushing her sandwich into the center of the table, her appetite suddenly gone.

"I'm not sure. They cleared the clinic and every floor above and below it first, then moved next door," he said. Knox lifted his sandwich absently, gaze trained on the window, as if he might see something his fellow deputies could not.

They stared in silence at the crowd outside, peppered with undercover deputies. Knox demolished his sandwich, while Jen held tight to her son. This could be the day she finally saw Madison again. She prayed with each passing moment her friend was still all right.

A sudden flash and resounding boom rattled the glass and caused the people outside to scream. Some ducked, bracing their hands over their heads. Others ran. Smoke billowed from the alley near the clinic.

D.J. jolted, then thrashed and cried.

Jen's ears rang. The air ripped from her lungs. Had she just witnessed an explosion?

Did she just lose Madison to a bomb?

Knox rose to his feet.

The windows of a building across the street were gone, broken and shattered. A dozen car alarms blared to life.

Knox cursed, cutting his attention between the frightening view outside and Jen as she moved to join him.

The chaos outside the café seemed to double as the moment of initial shock passed, and people began to panic.

"Go!" she said, rocking and clutching her frightened son. "Help them. We'll be right here." Terror slid like ice through her veins, chilling her from the inside out. Madison could have been near the blast. She could be one of the injured people. "Go!" Jen repeated when Knox didn't immediately move. "Be a hero." She forced a smile, worry for him sinking in as she realized what she'd asked.

A prolonged moment later, he dipped his chin and snapped into lawman mode. "Don't leave this building. Stay with the crowd. Call me if you see anything I need to know."

He waited for her nod of agreement, then broke into a sprint, weaving seamlessly through the cluster of patrons who'd moved to the window for a better look at the destruction.

Jen inched slowly away, back to the table where she'd sat with Knox before the blast.

Would there be another explosion?

Would the next one take Knox too?

The fire of panic burned up her neck and across her chest. It boiled in her gut and seized her breaths. The panic attacks she'd experienced regularly following the news of Dylan's death returned in full force, with one massive grip.

Until the blunt press of a gun barrel against her spine rocketed her straight back to clarity.

"This way," a low male voice instructed, wrapping an arm around her shoulders and leading her toward the back door. "Atta girl," he crooned. "You wouldn't want a bullet to make its way through you and into that sweet baby."

Chapter Twenty-Two

Knox raced across the street, stopping to check on drivers and passengers involved in fender benders as a result of the nearby explosion. "You okay?" he'd asked, knocking on windows and waiting for the stunned commuters to nod or respond verbally. "Hang tight," he told each victim. "Help is on the way."

He raised his phone and called dispatch, then gave a running tally of folks in need of assistance, issuing orders to bystanders and seeking signs of the black hats and windbreakers.

Where were all the deputies?

Sirens registered through the commotion. First responders were on their way.

"Winchester!" a familiar voice called through the dark acrid smoke.

Deputy Van appeared, moving in Knox's direction. "Looks like a Tannerite-induced explosion," he said. "Lots of noise. Broken windows. Some unfortunate projectile injuries." He squinted through the

hazy air at the fender benders and pedestrians un-
lucky enough to have been near the windows when
they shattered. "But the bulk of the damage was con-
tained. The explosives were set up in an unoccupied
portion of the building. No distinct signs anyone had
been there, but the area is still contaminated with de-
bris." He gripped the back of his neck, still visually
searching the streets. "I'm not sure what the point
was supposed to be. Some kind of distraction, maybe.
While he moved the missing woman?"

A pair of ambulances screamed their way into
view and parked as close to the destruction as possible, with complete disregard to signs for the tow-
away zone.

Knox stiffened as Van's words sank in, and he
swung his eyes to Coffee Cat, where he'd left two
very important people and a good chunk of his
heart. The reality of the situation hit him like a second bomb.

The explosion wasn't a distraction meant to cover
Martz's movement of Madison. It was meant to cover
the abduction of another woman altogether.

"Jen and her baby were in that coffee shop," Knox
said, breaking into a sprint without further explanation.

He flew back across the street, holding out one
arm to stop slow-moving vehicles as he cut around
their hoods and onto the packed sidewalk beyond. Too many minutes had passed since he'd left
her. How long had it been? Six? Eight? More? He

squeezed through the cluster of onlookers gathered in the café's open doorway, knocking shoulders and calling out apologies before landing soundly in the center of the small nearly vacated dining area.

Jen's panini and water sat on the table untouched.

She and D.J. were gone.

JEN HELD TIGHT to her son as Dr. Martz yanked her from the seat of his black sedan and shoved her forward, into the forest. A massive old house sat in the distance. Too far to reach without being shot by her abductor. Its dark windows and sunken porch suggested no one had likely lived there in a long while anyway. It wouldn't be a safe haven or refuge. Just a different place for her abductor to finish what he'd brought them there to do.

He'd parked the car on a deserted gravel lane, thickly lined in overgrown trees that obscured the county road. Pillars of crumbling brick stood near the mailbox, topped with an ugly urn-like sculpture and engraved with a word, maybe the owner's name, that age and neglect had nearly chiseled away.

"Move it," he demanded, nudging her shoulder once more.

Jen took baby steps, trying not to upset him while she scrambled to come up with an escape plan. She'd thought being driven away from town by a killer had been the most terrifying experience of her life. But walking into the forest with him was impossibly worse.

They'd driven for nearly an hour on unfamiliar country roads, passing very few homes and no notable landmarks.

If there was a blessing in the midst of her horror, it was that they'd arrived without incident, and D.J. had fallen asleep in her arms. The doctor's car had lacked a proper infant seat, and the combination of smooth roads and a car's engine had put her baby out like a light.

The irony of a safe arrival to the destination of their intended demise wasn't lost on Jen, but she appreciated it anyway.

Martz had been silent, but fidgety, as he drove, checking his rearview mirror often and watching her intermittently. He let the handgun resting on his lap speak for him.

Jen shuffled forward, nudged regularly by Martz's gun, and D.J. blew spit bubbles and babbled against her chest as she panicked internally. She eyeballed fallen limbs and sizable rocks, wondering if she could reach and swing one at her captor before he could manage an accurate shot.

Ultimately, she didn't dare try.

Tears stung her eyes as she imagined what might happen next with each crunch of fallen leaves underfoot. Only the darkest, most horrid things came to mind. "You don't have to do this," she whispered, willing herself to speak for the first time since Martz had found her in the café. She hadn't wanted to provoke him before, but the time for plotting an escape was up. She had to try anything she could, and talking to him was her only option.

"Shut up and keep walking," he said quietly, a note of regret in his tone. "I should've just shot you the night you drove through the park looking for Madison. This could've been over days ago."

"I won't tell anyone what happened," she pressed, ignoring his demands. "I swear it. You might hurt my baby if I tell, so I would never. You can leave us here in the woods. Get a head start on leaving town and evading the sheriff's department. Start over somewhere else. I don't have a phone." Martz had made sure of that. He'd chucked her cell phone through his car window before they'd ever left town. "I can't call for help," she continued. "It will take me forever to make my way back to civilization."

"Shut. Up," he repeated, breaking the words into two sharp sentences.

The car shrank behind them, and her fear grew. "What are you going to do to us?" she asked, knowing and hating the obvious answer. "You don't have to add two more murders to your charges. Killing your partner and receptionist was bad enough. Killing a baby isn't going to help things when they catch you, which they will if you don't leave us here and get out of town."

"I haven't killed anyone," Martz said, scanning the forest with a solemn gaze. "I didn't tamper with Katie's car. Robert did. And I didn't kill him. He was a junkie, hooked on his own drug. I just put him in his car to buy myself time to think. A lot of good that did me," he grouched. "Autopsies are supposed to take weeks. I don't know why all of this is going wrong."

Jen fought the urge to scream as her mind raced to process his claims. "Dr. Abel was the one selling MX-10?"

"He's the mastermind," Martz said, begrudgingly. "The creator, distributor and user. It was supposed to supplement his income after he was taken to the cleaners in his divorce. He'd been making the pills for himself for years, which was probably why his wife left him in the first place." Martz shook his head. "I was an idiot for agreeing to let him handle business through our practice. Now he's dead and I'm left holding the bag."

A measure of hope rose in her. If Martz wasn't the cold-blooded killer she thought he was, would he still shoot her and her child if they tried to run?

The hope collapsed as she imagined making an attempted escape.

Even if Martz hadn't killed Katie or Abel, he was undoubtedly the one who'd attacked Jen at her apartment. The familiar spearmint scent on his clothing had turned her stomach as they'd driven, and it hung heavy in the air between them now.

"What did you do to Madison?" she asked, pressing the words around a painful lump in her throat. "She's my best friend, and I don't understand what happened."

He ignored her, and she pressed on.

"Please. I need to know."

Martz moved to stand in front of her, blocking her path and pointing the gun at her face.

Her hands flew up on instinct, and she turned her back to him, putting herself between the gun and her baby.

Rustling leaves and brush drew her attention over one shoulder.

Behind her, Martz dropped a mass of vines and branches onto the ground, revealing a rusted metal door set in a small embankment. Probably an old storm shelter belonging to the decrepit farmhouse she'd seen. He stuffed the gun into his waistband and gave her a firm look. "Don't try anything, or I'll hurt him." His gaze dropped to her middle, where her arms wound over D.J., still angled out of Martz's sight.

He removed a padlock, then heaved the creaking door wide with effort and pointed into the blackened tomb. "Get in."

Jen gaped and considered her escape options once more. She wouldn't make it back to the car or road before he shot her. But if she went inside, would she ever get out? "What is it?" she asked, the question blurting from her lips.

Where was he putting her? What was in there? And how long could she and her baby survive without food or water?

"Watch your step," he said, ignoring her question.

"Don't make me force you, the way I forced your friend. She wasn't carrying a baby."

Jen stilled. Her gaze drifted to the dark hollow. "You brought Madison here? Is she still in there?" How many days had it been? Could she still be alive?

His grimace turned to exhaustion as he motioned with his gun. "I won't ask nicely again."

Jen didn't doubt him, so she steeled her nerves and took a step inside.

The door slammed behind her, and D.J. cried.

She shushed her baby in the darkness, listening as the metal lock clanged against the door, being returned to its place. Then she turned in the impossible blackness, afraid of what awaited her and recalling Martz's mention of Madison. "Hello?" she whispered, listening intently for sounds of another person, and hopefully nothing else.

A low moan and strange scratching sound answered back. A moment later, a cough.

"Madison?" Jen pressed her palms to the cool cement walls and used one pointed foot to feel for steps. She counted four wooden treads, committing each to memory in case she needed to backtrack in a hurry.

On solid ground again, she concentrated on the scratchy sound, both familiar and not. And let the small glow of light draw her forward.

The air was cool and earthen, raising gooseflesh on her arms and assaulting her senses.

"Madison?" Jen asked again, trailing her fingertips along the wall. She sang quietly to calm D.J. and distract her own panicked mind.

The scratching sound began again, and the light slowly brightened.

Madison's dark form came into view, curled on the ground, head resting on one arm like a pillow.

"Maddie!" Jen rushed to her friend's side and lowered herself to her knees, elated and terrified at the sight of her. "What happened? Are you hurt?"

Madison's filthy face and closed eyes made the second question unnecessary.

Something was very wrong.

"Hey," she tried again, stroking hair from her friend's overheated cheeks.

Madison twitched her hand, and the sound began again. A small crankshaft light glowed in Madison's fist, storing energy and creating light with every grip and release of her hand.

Had she been doing that all these days? Just to stop the darkness?

"You shouldn't be here," Madison said. "Take D.J. away."

Jen nearly sobbed in relief and horror as she snuggled her still-whimpering son. "I can't. Martz locked us in. Now we have to find a way out."

Madison grimaced. "I think I broke my leg. He pushed me down the steps. I hit my head and landed on something sharp. I might have a concussion. My leg's hot, infected, I think."

Jen bit her lip as she recalled the heat in Madison's

cheek. She settled a hand on her forehead for confirmation. Her friend was burning. "May I?" Jen asked, taking the light from Madison's weak grip.

Jen squeezed the crank fast and hard, captivating D.J.'s attention and bringing the small glow into maximum brilliance behind the aged plastic shield. She swept the light over her roommate's curled body, lingering on her red and swollen leg. Jogging shorts revealed a deep gash on the thigh above the knee. Whatever she'd been cut with had left a serious wound, and there was no doubt about the infection. "Okay," Jen said. "Time to get out of here."

Madison coughed, then groaned. "The door is locked. I tried."

Jen powered up the hand crank, keeping her rhythm steady and moving the cone of light around the room. "What do we have to work with?"

"Not much," Madison whispered, her eyes drifting shut once more. "I drank the little water I could find. I'm sorry."

"You did the right thing," Jen said, mentally adding dehydration to the tally of injuries and issues with her friend.

A set of rickety wooden shelves clung to one wall, angled, as if they might give up their load of ancient canned goods at any moment. A decrepit table, covered in mildewed papers and books, stood a few feet away, an open first aid kit on top. Madison had likely rifled through the kit once she was able to find it, before infection had set in.

Jen turned in a circle, illuminating an empty jug on its side near Madison's head, presumably the water she'd consumed. She cringed at the thought of her friend's fear, pain and despair. To be alone in the dark, injured and hurting. Hungry and fevered. She couldn't imagine what Madison had been through, and she needed to get them out of there.

Madison coughed, and Jen returned to her, revving the hand crank for light. "I'm so sorry you and D.J. were pulled into this," Madison rasped. "I tried so hard to keep you out of it."

"I'm not caught," Jen said, mustering as much bravery as she could manage. "I'm rescuing you."

Madison gave a small brittle laugh. "I didn't know what to do when I realized the doctors were making and selling MX-10. I took some pills home as evidence to help prove my story, but I got scared. I waited too long to call the police." Her voice went thin, and she stopped to cough some more, before pressing on. "Once Martz came for me, I couldn't shake him. I ran to the park and hid, but he had a gun. I knew he'd kill me. I tried to leave a list of the people involved. People they'd hurt or sold to, but I didn't get to finish my note." Fresh tears ran silently over her cheeks. "I botched everything. Now look at us."

Jen squared her shoulders. "You haven't botched anything," she said. "This isn't over." She could save them. She just had to think.

"Madison?" she asked, gaze falling on the badly

infected cut on her friend's thigh. "What did you cut yourself on?"

"I'm not sure," she rasped. "It was dark. I found my way in here, then felt around for another door. I found the flashlight, first aid kit and water. Then I lay down to rest my head and things got fuzzy."

Jen moved back toward the shelter's entrance.

"Don't leave," Madison called, her voice suddenly panicked.

"I'm not leaving," Jen promised. "I want to see what you fell on. I need something to break us out of here. The shelves might work, if I can take them apart. A shovel or something metal would be better."

"Take me," Madison pleaded. "I don't want to be in the dark."

Jen doubled back and knelt beside Madison, who looped a fevered arm across her shoulders. "Ready?" she asked.

Madison screamed as Jen tried to hoist her upright.

"Okay," she whispered, consoling Madison and D.J. at once. "Wait." She lowered Madison to the ground and let her take deep breaths. Jen collected the newspapers and spread them on the ground at Madison's side. "Can you roll onto your side?" she asked.

Madison complied with effort, and the opened papers became a pathetic makeshift backboard.

"I'm going to try to drag you," she said. "I'll go slow, and I'll stop if it hurts." She handed the light to Madison, then dipped into a squat.

D.J. huffed and complained, cheeks red and bottom lip jutted.

Jen gripped the ancient papers and tugged gently, until Madison began to move.

One small step at a time, they made their way toward the stairs, adjusting and replacing sheets of paper as needed, until they reached their destination.

She fell onto the ground at Madison's side, kissing D.J. and panting from effort. "Well, that was easy," she said.

Madison moaned. "My leg is definitely broken."

"But you're alive," Jen said. "The sheriff's department has been looking for you, and there's a manhunt underway for Martz. We're going to be okay. We just have to get out of here, so we can be found." She pulled the crank light from Madison's grip and swept the area.

An overturned metal box came into view against the far wall.

"Bingo." She hurried to see what was inside. The container was empty, but her eyes misted with hope and relief at the sight of a single long screwdriver lying nearby.

Jen pulled D.J. from the sling and returned to Madison's side. She spread the sling on the cold dirty floor like a blanket, and lay D.J. on top. "I need you to stay awake and protect him," she said to her friend. "Can you do that for me one more time?"

Madison chuckled, then moaned. "You just got here. You already want a babysitter?"

"It's not as if you're doing anything else," Jen said, smiling as she faced the rusty door. The metal was in bad shape along the edges and ground, deteriorating from age and weather. She could definitely work with that.

Jen jammed the business end of the tool into the worst-looking section of metal and levered a chunk of rust away. A pinhole of light shined through, and she turned to share the joy with her friend.

But Madison had tipped over beside D.J., her eyes closed and face slack.

Jen had to work faster.

Madison's survival depended on it.

Chapter Twenty-Three

Knox kicked the dumpster outside Coffee Cat and fought the urge to scream.

The commotion out front had drawn attention for blocks, but the real devastation had occurred silently and without notice. Martz had walked into the coffee shop and ushered Jen and D.J. away. No one had even noticed. All eyes and phone cameras were focused on the fender benders and smoke. If not for security cameras at a bank on the opposite end of the block, there would've been no indication about what had happened to Jen and her baby.

Even now, knowing who'd taken them, there was little to suggest where they'd gone.

Every deputy in Jefferson County was on the look-out for the black sedan. The car's temporary license plate number, a fake, on a car registered to someone in another town, was thankfully picked up by bank cameras. A description of the vehicle and passengers had been broadcast to highway patrol across the region. And like her roommate before her, no one had a clue where Jen had gone.

"All right," Derek said, stepping into Knox's strike zone and pushing his phone into view. "I've got something. There's a property about an hour from here that was owned by Martz's granny before it passed to his mom, who uses a different last name. The mom lives in Phoenix, so the house is family owned and, as far as I can tell, empty. Local patrols have been dispatched. It's a long shot, but right now it's all we've got to go on, and you look like you're about to combust. I'm going to check it out. You want to come along?"

Knox nodded. "Yeah." He reached for the phone, to get a closer look at the map, while he followed Derek to his truck. "I can't keep standing around here when they could be getting farther away every second."

The cousins were on the road within minutes and cruising away from town.

Knox changed the view on the map of the property in question, trading an overview of general directions for a satellite view. He zoomed and scrolled the immediate area. "An abandoned home seems like a good place to store a couple of missing women."

Derek grunted. "I thought the same thing. Wouldn't be a bad place to set up a drug enterprise either."

Knox stilled as a broken-down and faded sign became visible on the small screen. The paint was chipped and the wooden frame barely standing, but the remnants of words and familiar green leaves tightened the knots in his stomach. "Was this place previously a mint farm?"

Derek shot him a questioning look, gaze dropping briefly to the cell phone. "His mother's family raised mint before the whole industry moved to the Pacific Northwest, but that was more than sixty years ago. How'd you guess that from the satellite view? I only found the information by happenchance while confirming it was his mother's property."

Knox traded Derek's device for his own, dialing dispatch with purpose. "The gunman in Jen's apartment smelled like mint."

JEN GRIPPED THE baby sling with both hands and hefted it from the floor. She'd filled the material with the heaviest cans of ancient food she could find, and broken away as much of the rusted door as possible. Now, it was time to get out of there.

"One," she said, swinging the sling for momentum. "Two. Three." She swung the makeshift battering ram against the door with a body-jolting thud. The metal groaned and strained under the hit.

"Again," Madison said, before beginning to cough once more.

Madison had moved in and out of consciousness throughout the day, oscillating between speech and incoherency, her fever seeming to rise.

D.J. cried continually. He was wet, hungry and

scared, but Jen couldn't help him. She couldn't help any of them without her bag of well-planned emergency staples. What good had all the hours of forethought done her when something like this had happened? Just like the bomb that had taken Dylan and Bob, there hadn't been any way to prepare for this.

So, she swung.

The sound and impact reverberated down her arms and spine. Her joints ached and her muscles protested. Her head hummed with the dull pain of physical and mental exertion.

Again, she told herself. *Again*. And she swung.

And she swung.

And she swung.

A great shifting screech broke through the cascade of desperate sobs and tears, sending her back down the steps at a run.

A large section of metal gave way, collapsing inward and falling toward her.

"Whoa! Whoa! Whoa!" She leaped down the steps and dove at her son and Madison, shielding them with her body and taking the brunt of the collision with her back. Her hands planted on the wall where Madison's back rested, her knees dug into the floor.

D.J. remained, miraculously, untouched in the space beneath Jen's arched torso.

Pain screamed up Jen's back and shoulders, the sharp rusty edges of the panel surely taking skin and flesh in the attack.

Her son's cries filled her ears as she shifted the heavy metal away and rested her head on the filthy floor beside D.J.

The dimming crank light lay under the steps, fallen and nearly forgotten.

Moonlight and fresh minty air rolled in through the hole above them.

KNOX EXITED DEREK'S truck at a run, grabbing the first uniformed person he saw and demanding details.

According to the local detective, a search party had just arrived and was dividing to explore the eighty-acre property, on foot and with all-terrain vehicles, but the encroaching night would be a problem. The house had been confirmed empty by the initial set of dispatched officers, but a set of recent tire marks were visible upon their arrival. The detective confirmed the tracks were likely made by a sedan or other midsized car.

Knox scrubbed anxious hands over his head and locked them there, elbows pointed skyward and a desperate prayer in his heart. Jen was determined and resourceful. If there was a way to signal searchers for rescue, she would find one. *Where are you?* he asked silently, willing the night to give her up.

Eighty acres was a formidable amount of land to search in the best of conditions. Twilight had made things more complicated.

A sea of spotlights bobbed and swam in the fields

near the old farmhouse. The first sets of volunteers
and lawmen were beginning their hunt.

A chill in the air raised the hairs on Knox's arms
and climbed up the back of his neck. The scent of
spearmint rose on the breeze like an apparition.

And in the distance, a small fragile cry reached
Knox's ears.

"D.J."

JEN HUGGED HER baby to her chest as she dragged herself up the wooden stairs and into the night.

Madison lay on the floor behind her, unconscious,
as she had been since Jen reopened her eyes after
the hit with falling metal. Madison hadn't responded
to Jen's pleas, and the impossibility of dragging her
up the steps on newspaper had forced Jen's hand.
She didn't want to leave her friend behind, but she
also couldn't sit and wait for rescue. As it was, she
didn't know if Madison would survive. Every hour
and every minute counted.

Jen willed her feet to move, the piercing pain from
her injured back cutting deeper with every step. She
couldn't find the voice to comfort D.J., so she held
him more tightly as he screamed, hoping he could feel
her love, even if she was in too much pain to speak.

Every inch of progress took her farther from Madison and farther from the horrid tomb where they'd
been left to die. But the oppressing darkness of the
nighttime forest felt almost worse. She was alone
now, and this new tomb was vast. What if she wan-

dered in the wrong direction? What if she became hopelessly lost?

What if she failed them all?

Her tears fell on D.J.'s hair, and she stifled a sob.

It was time for her to be strong.

The thunder of footfalls froze her in place, and for a minute she imagined Martz returning. Could he have come to check on them? And if so, would he let them live if he found they'd escaped?

Pinpricks of lights appeared on her right, dancing like fireflies over distant fields, barely visible through the dense forest trees. Was she hallucinating?

She stared at the lights, wondering if she should go toward them or maintain her path. Uncertainty rooted her, confused her, terrified her. A wrong choice could cost lives.

And then, above the screech of her wailing son, she heard her name.

Knox jogged toward the sound of D.J.'s cries, his heart in his throat, and his cousin at his side. A dozen volunteers and local law enforcement followed.

"Jen!" he called.

Derek echoed her name, and the others behind them did the same.

The forest was dark and treacherous, impossible to see clearly or navigate properly, even with the mass of flashlights in his rescue party. He couldn't imagine doing it alone, with a baby and no light source.

Heavy brush slapped his legs and briars caught on his jeans as he ran, calling her name with every breath.

They took wrong turns, following the sounds of D.J.'s muffled cries, distorted by trees and distance. Until suddenly the wails grew louder.

They were on the right track and Knox ran harder, faster, determined to reach her before she spent another moment scared and alone.

Then suddenly, Jen called back.

JEN OPENED HER eyes to the offensive fluorescent lighting of her hospital room. She'd been treated to nonstop check-ins from medical staff and nosy but well-meaning Winchesters since her admission the night before.

D.J. had been examined and released into the custody of Knox's auntie and uncle when Knox had refused to leave Jen's side. His aunt and uncle had nearly needed resuscitation from overwhelming joy. Jen had been a little drugged at the time, but she thought she'd seen Auntie Rosa skipping away.

"Good morning," a husky voice said, yawning deeply after the greeting. Knox shifted in the utilitarian hospital chair beside her, attempting to get comfortable. His hair was tousled and his cheeks were dark with two days of stubble. His clothes still smelled of the outdoors, but thankfully not of spearmint.

"Hey," she whispered, falling deep into his kind green eyes. "You didn't have to stay."

He leaned forward, pushing hair from her fore-head and planting a kiss in its place. "You're here," he said. "Where else would I be?"

She smiled, and Knox exhaled.

"How do you feel?" he asked.

"Better than her," Jen said, shifting her gaze over his shoulder, to the bed where Madison slept. A dozen machines beeped and blinked around her. IV bags hung from multiple hooks, each running necessities direct to her veins. "She almost died," Jen whispered. "Dehydration. Sepsis. A broken ankle and tibia."

Madison's surgery had taken hours. Her leg had needed to be re-broken and reset. The infection in her thigh had spread severely and nearly killed her. The concussion had been the least of her many problems, and the emotional trauma from her experience would likely be around long after she'd physically healed.

Knox tipped his head, bringing his face back into Jen's view. "She's alive because of you."

"We're all safe because of you," she challenged.

He wrinkled his nose. "Technically, Derek deserves the credit for finding Martz's family property," he said, "but we never would've found you or that storm cellar at night if you hadn't done what you did. And Madison wouldn't have made it until morning."

A single hot tear formed at the corner of Jen's eye.

Knox swept it away with the pad of his thumb. "Martz was caught near the state line. He's in custody, and given the extent of his crimes, he won't be free again for a very long time."

"Good." She nodded.

Knox smiled, but the expression grew tentative. "I think you and D.J. should stay with me while you heal. At least until Madison is released. You can rest and let me take care of you awhile before you go home and try to meet all of your friend's needs too."

Jen glanced at her friend once more. "Her folks are coming for her," she said. "They'll be here this afternoon."

"Then I guess you can stay with me as long as you want," Knox said.

He raised her hand in his and kissed her fingers. "I hate that you're hurt, but I'm so grateful the metal that damaged your back didn't break it. You should've seen yourself when we found you. I thought you'd been shot."

There'd been a lot more blood than Jen had realized before being hoisted into the ambulance. Under proper lighting, the gore was real, and she couldn't even see the wounds on her back.

The three-by-four-foot piece of door that chased her down the shelter steps had ripped large sections of skin away from her back and left deep cuts that had required extensive stitches. She'd received skin grafts too, but the injuries weren't nearly as bad as they could've been. And she was eternally thankful D.J. hadn't been harmed at all. Not a single bruise or scratch on his perfect little self. That was all that really mattered.

Knox stroked her hand with warm fingers. "I thought I'd lost you," he said. "I know it's probably too soon to say this, but I wasn't sure what I'd do without you," he said. "You feel like the missing piece to a puzzle I thought I'd finished."

Jen's throat constricted, and her chest ached at his welcomed words. "And D.J.?" she asked, unable to return his confession with the truth of her heart until she heard the whole story. Because she wasn't just one person anymore, and the smaller, handsomer part of her was far more important than the rest.

Knox frowned, and her stomach dropped. "Didn't he tell you?" Knox asked.

Jen pressed her lips and shook her head, smashing the bubble of hope and waiting for his explanation.

"D.J. and I already talked about this," he said. "While you were sleeping, we negotiated arrangements for the bigger bedroom. I won, since I plan to share it with you, and that just makes sense. He agreed, but is demanding to meet the other kids in this family before making a final decision, and he's asked me to get him out of that nasty mush you feed him for breakfast. Beyond that, he says he trusts your judgment."

Jen covered her mouth as emotions began to rise once more. "It's not too soon," she whispered. "I feel it too, and I want to be with you. Long after I've healed," she said. "Way, way after."

Knox's brows rose. "You sure about that?"

She nodded, the motion feeling erratic and wild.

"You sure it's not just the IV talking?" he asked. "Because I'm thinking the three of us can get a really long-term situation going."

She bobbed her head again, speechless and reaching for him.

Knox rose to lean over her. He stroked her cheek and tipped their foreheads together. "I love you," he said, then kissed her lips with adoration.

She relaxed into the perfect moment, enveloped in his precious words.

A commotion in the hall spread her lips into a smile. "Visitors?" she asked.

Knox checked over his shoulder, then turned back with a pleased expression. "Yeah."

"Your family?" she guessed.

"Maybe soon," he said. "If you're interested in my offer, I've got something I need to ask your dad."

"Baby!" Jen's mother called, rushing past Knox to her daughter's side.

Her father trailed behind, a look of distress and relief mixing on his brow. He stopped to shake Knox's hand. "Thank you for calling," he said. "It was awful nice of your family to arrange our airfare. We couldn't think straight after receiving this news."

"Of course," Knox answered. "She's quite a hero. I know she's been missing you both, and while I wish the circumstances were different, I'm glad you're here."

"Mama?" Jen asked, receiving an onslaught of hugs and kisses, as if she were a child.

Then Jen remembered what it felt like to be a mother, and she hugged hers back a little more tightly.

Epilogue

D.J. toddled over the warm dry sand in dress shorts, a white button-down shirt, bare feet and suspenders. The pageboy hat his grandpa had placed on his head only a few minutes before sat painfully askew.

"That hat is coming off," Jen whispered.

Her father chuckled. "Look at him go. He's a natural beach boy. I'll bet he's one heck of a swimmer."

D.J. face-planted, as if on cue, and the hat rolled into the sand.

"He's a total tadpole," she agreed. "He's still getting his land legs."

Her dad laughed and set his hand on her fingers resting in the crook of his arm. "I'm glad you're here," he said, eyes misty and full of emotion, the way they'd been when he'd arrived in her hospital room, nearly a year before.

"My folks live here," she said sweetly, setting a palm against his smooth cheek. "Where else would I be?"

Those words had meant everything to her when

Knox had first said them, and she'd made it her mission to live by them. From now on, she would always be where her family needed her. And today, they needed her on this beach. Her father's health severely limited his ability to travel, so she'd volunteered to come to him.

Thankfully, Knox's family shared his motto, and they had no problems traveling. They didn't even mind baking in the hot Florida sun.

Before her, three rows of ten chairs each had been arranged in the sand outside her favorite resort. An aisle divided the guests but not the people. Her mom held Auntie Rosa's hand in the front row. Uncle Hank swept a crawling D.J. into his arms and shook the fallen hat before placing it back onto his head. Then he flew Jen's son like an airplane to the grapevine altar laced with white silk and roses.

"Are you ready?" her father asked, voice cracking on the words.

"I am," she said, tightening her hold on his arm. "I love you, Daddy. And I love him too."

His expression crumbled at her gentle use of the childhood endearment. "I know you do, baby girl. If I didn't, I wouldn't let you go."

With that, the music changed, and they began their walk past family and friends.

Madison accepted Jen's bouquet when she arrived. Her deep blue dress sparkled against the matching sea behind her. She'd made a full recovery, and moved back to Missouri, where her parents had overseen her care. And she'd met a professional football player, also in recovery, treating his blown-out knee. Maybe she was just a sucker for uniforms, because they would be married at Christmas.

Knox's green eyes flashed as he drank her in before taking her hands. "You're beautiful," he whispered, and her cheeks heated with pleasure.

Their exchange of vows stole her breath, almost as completely as the man before her had stolen her heart.

"I now pronounce you," the pastor declared, "husband and wife."

A chorus of cheers went up before them.

The line of groomsmen at Knox's back, Cruz, Blaze, Lucas, Derek and the last remaining Winchester bachelor, Nash, gave a collective "whoop!"

Madison and the groomsmen's wives clapped and cheered.

The guests rose and began to scatter.

Across the sand behind the altar, a gaggle of children ran wild, and precariously close to the surf, monitored by four delighted grandparents and an army of loved ones, hurrying to catch their offspring.

"Welcome to the circus," Knox whispered, planting a much deeper and more intimate kiss on Jen's lips as they stood alone at the altar.

The pastor took his cue and slipped away.

Jen pulled back, arms draped over her husband's shoulders. "I believe this is Winchester Country," she corrected, marveling at her incredibly good fortune.

"What do you think about a few minutes alone before the reception?"

"Alone?" Knox bent immediately and swept her off her feet, into his arms. "It's the only thing I've thought about since you showed up in that dress."

She laughed.

"If we make a run for it, we might have six or seven minutes before anyone notices we're gone," he said, breaking into a jog.

She giggled and buried her face into his neck. "Actually, I assigned each of my bridesmaids a task that will waylay and detain the family for a minimum of thirty minutes."

Knox growled with pleasure as he pressed the elevator button with gusto. "Another reason I love you, Mrs. Winchester," he said, backing her into the empty car when it arrived. "My smart, sexy little Scout."

She arched against him as the elevator rocketed them upward. "Wait until you see what I've got in my honeymoon bag," she teased, certain no amount of time alone with him would ever be long enough.

* * * * *

To Catch a Killer, *the final book in
award-winning author Julie Anne Lindsey's
Heartland Heroes miniseries,
goes on sale next month!*

*And in case you missed the previous books
in the series, look for:*

SVU Surveillance
Protecting His Witness
Kentucky Crime Ring
Stay Hidden

Wherever Harlequin Intrigue books are sold!

Get 4 FREE REWARDS!

We'll send you 2 FREE Books plus 2 FREE Mystery Gifts.

FREE Value Over **$20**

Both the **Harlequin Intrigue®** and **Harlequin® Romantic Suspense** series feature compelling novels filled with heart-racing action-packed romance that will keep you on the edge of your seat.

YES! Please send me 2 FREE novels from the Harlequin Intrigue or Harlequin Romantic Suspense series and my 2 FREE gifts (gifts are worth about $10 retail). After receiving them, if I don't wish to receive any more books, I can return the shipping statement marked "cancel." If I don't cancel, I will receive 6 brand-new Harlequin Intrigue Larger-Print books every month and be billed just $5.99 each in the U.S. or $6.49 each in Canada, a savings of at least 14% off the cover price or 4 brand-new Harlequin Romantic Suspense books every month and be billed just $4.99 each in the U.S. or $5.74 each in Canada, a savings of at least 13% off the cover price. It's quite a bargain! Shipping and handling is just 50¢ per book in the U.S. and $1.25 per book in Canada.* I understand that accepting the 2 free books and gifts places me under no obligation to buy anything. I can always return a shipment and cancel at any time. The free books and gifts are mine to keep no matter what I decide.

Choose one: ☐ **Harlequin Intrigue**
Larger-Print
(199/399 HDN GNXC)

☐ **Harlequin Romantic Suspense**
(240/340 HDN GNMZ)

Name (please print)

Address   Apt. #

City   State/Province   Zip/Postal Code

Email: Please check this box ☐ if you would like to receive newsletters and promotional emails from Harlequin Enterprises ULC and its affiliates. You can unsubscribe anytime.

Mail to the Harlequin Reader Service:
IN U.S.A.: P.O. Box 1341, Buffalo, NY 14240-8531
IN CANADA: P.O. Box 603, Fort Erie, Ontario L2A 5X3

Want to try 2 free books from another series? Call 1-800-873-8635 or visit www.ReaderService.com.

---

*Terms and prices subject to change without notice. Prices do not include sales taxes, which will be charged (if applicable) based on your state or country of residence. Canadian residents will be charged applicable taxes. Offer not valid in Quebec. This offer is limited to one order per household. Books received may not be as shown. Not valid for current subscribers to the Harlequin Intrigue or Harlequin Romantic Suspense series. All orders subject to approval. Credit or debit balances in a customer's account(s) may be offset by any other outstanding balance owed by or to the customer. Please allow 4 to 6 weeks for delivery. Offer available while quantities last.

Your Privacy—Your information is being collected by Harlequin Enterprises ULC, operating as Harlequin Reader Service. For a complete summary of the information we collect, how we use this information and to whom it is disclosed, please visit our privacy notice located at corporate.harlequin.com/privacy-notice. From time to time we may also exchange your personal information with reputable third parties. If you wish to opt out of this sharing of your personal information, please visit readerservice.com/consumerschoice or call 1-800-873-8635. **Notice to California Residents**—Under California law, you have specific rights to control and access your data. For more information on these rights and how to exercise them, visit corporate.harlequin.com/california-privacy.

HIHRS22

#2067 SNIFFING OUT DANGER
K-9s on Patrol • by Elizabeth Heiter

When former big-city cop Ava Callan stumbles upon a bomb, she seizes the chance to prove herself to the small-town police department where she's becoming a K-9 handler...but especially to charming lead investigator Eli Thorne. The only thing more explosive than her chemistry with the out-of-town captain? The danger menacing them at every turn...

#2068 UNDERCOVER COUPLE
A Ree and Quint Novel • by Barb Han

Legendary ATF agent Quint Casey isn't thrilled to pose as Ree Sheppard's husband for a covert investigation into a weapons ring that could be tied to his past. But when his impetuous "wife" proves her commitment to the job, Quint feels a spark just as alarming as the dangerous killers he's sworn to unmask.

#2069 DODGING BULLETS IN BLUE VALLEY
A North Star Novel Series • by Nicole Helm

When the attempted rescue of his infant twins goes horribly wrong, Blue Valley sheriff Garret Averly and North Star doctor Betty Wagner take the mission into their own hands. Deep in the Montana mountains and caught in a deadly storm, he's willing to sacrifice everything to bring Betty and his children home safely.

#2070 TO CATCH A KILLER
Heartland Heroes • by Julie Anne Lindsey

Apprehending a violent fugitive is US marshal Nash Winchester's top priority when Great Falls chef Lana Iona becomes the next target as the sole eyewitness to a murder. Forced to stay constantly on the move, can the Kentucky lawman stop a killer from permanently silencing the woman he's never forgotten?

#2071 ACCIDENTAL AMNESIA
The Saving Kelby Creek Series • by Tyler Anne Snell

Awakening in an ambulance headed to Kelby Creek, Melanie Blankenship can't remember why or how she got there. While she's back in the town that turned on her following her ex-husband's shocking scandal, evidence mounts against Mel in a deadly crime. Can her former love Deputy Sterling Costner uncover the criminal before she pays the ultimate price?

#2072 THE BODY IN THE WALL
A Badge of Courage Novel • by Rita Herron

The sooner Special Agent Macy Stark can sell her childhood home, the sooner she can escape her small town and shameful past—until she discovers a body in the wall and her childhood nightmares return. Handsome local sheriff Stone Lawson joins the cold case—but someone will stop at nothing to keep the past hidden.

SPECIAL EXCERPT FROM

HQN

*Sheriff Matt Corbin never expected to return to
his hometown of Last Ridge, Texas. Nor did he ever
imagine he'd be reunited with his childhood crush,
Emory Parkman, a successful wedding-dress designer
who's been even unluckier in love than Matt. And yet
there she is, living on the family ranch he now owns...
and working just as hard as he is to fight the attraction
that's only getting stronger by the day...*

Read on for a sneak peek of
Summer at Stallion Ridge,
part of the Last Ride, Texas, series
from USA TODAY *bestselling author Delores Fossen.*

"I wouldn't have bought the place if I'd known you would ever
come back here to live," she explained. "You always said you'd
get out and stay out, come hell or high water."

Yeah, he'd indeed said that all right. Now he was eating
those words. "Anything else going on with you that I should
know about?"

"I'm making Natalie's wedding dress," she readily admitted.

Maybe she thought she'd see some disapproval on his face
over that. She wouldn't. Matt didn't necessarily buy into the
bunk about Emory's dresses being *mostly lucky*, but he wanted
Natalie to be happy. Because that in turn would improve Jack's
chances of being happy. If Vince Parkman and Last Ride were
what Natalie needed for that happiness, then Matt was willing to
give the man, and the town, his blessing.

"Anything else?" he pressed. "I'd like not to get blindsided
by something else for at least the next twenty-four hours."

Emory cocked her head to the side, studying him again.

PHDFEXP0322

Then smiling. Not a big beaming smile but one with a sly edge to it. "You mean like nightly loud parties, nude gardening or weddings in the pasture?"

Of course, his brain, and another stupid part of him, latched right on to the nude gardening. The breeze didn't help, either, because it swirled her dress around again, this time lifting it up enough for him to get a glimpse of her thigh.

Her smile widened. "No loud parties, weddings in the pasture and I'll keep nude gardening to a minimum." She stuck out her hand. "Want to shake on that?"

Matt was sure he was frowning, but it had nothing to do with the truce she obviously wanted. It was because he was trying to figure out how the hell he was going to look out the kitchen window and not get a too-clear image of Emory naked except for gardening gloves.

He shook his head, but because the stupid part of him was still playing into this, his gaze locked on her mouth. That mouth he suddenly wanted to taste.

"The last time I kissed you, your brothers saw it and beat me up. Repeatedly," he grumbled.

No way had he intended to say that aloud. It'd just popped out. Of course, no way had he wanted to have the urge to kiss Emory, either.

"It's not a good idea for us to be living so close to each other," Matt managed to add.

"Don't worry," she said, her voice a sexy siren's purr. "You'll never even notice I'm here." With a smile that was the perfect complement to that purr, she fluttered her fingers in a little wave, turned and walked toward the cottage.

Matt just stood there, knowing that what she'd said was a Texas-sized lie. Oh, yeah, he would notice all right.

Don't miss
Summer at Stallion Ridge
by Delores Fossen, available April 2022 wherever
HQN books and ebooks are sold.

HQNBooks.com

PHDFEXP0322